moon
trees
and
other
orphans

moon
trees
and
other
orphans

Leigh Camacho Rourks

 Black
Lawrence
Press

Black
Lawrence
Press

www.blacklawrence.com

Executive Editor: Diane Goettel
Book Design: Amy Freels
Cover Design: Zoe Norvell

Published 2019 by Black Lawrence Press.
Printed in the United States.

For Lee,
my first reader, my research partner,
my cheerleader, my travel buddy, my best friend,
and my love.

You rocks my socks.

Contents

Moon Trees

Stute's heels clipped my toes as he rocked back, half in and half out of the doorway to our apartment. He was ten then. I was eighteen. I had my hand on his back, and I could feel how stiff his small, hard muscles turned, as if he was clinching everything. The word "um" cracked out of him, just a splinter of his little voice. Liminal moment. I should have run. I should have left right then. I should have grabbed my little brother and hauled his skinny ass away, taken a train right out of Louisiana. Sometimes at night I whisper it: I should have. I should have. Making my voice the wheels of a train. I had enough money in tips saved that we probably could have just run.

Maybe we could have, anyway.

I didn't need to know what he saw in there. I didn't need to look past the door frame. I knew "Um." I knew that sound, that squeak. I knew it meant we were about to cross the threshold into crazy.

It was not new to me, the world on the other side of that door.

I have known it my whole life. It has been everything.

When I was small, my mother would sometimes tuck me into her lap and tell me how Stuart Roosa flew an unborn forest round and round the moon in 1971 and then sprinkled the earth with it. Her voice was always earnest, every sentence a sacred truth. I can tell you word for word the story of my mother finding one of those seeds and hiding it in a locket. I can tell you how one day, when she was very lonely, she gobbled that seed

1

up to make me. When I was a child, I did not fall asleep to Cinderella's broom strokes and ballroom dancing. Instead, my mother told me of how her fish-white belly, iridescent with life, grew heavy and cratered with my weight. I branched out inside of her, and my fetal limbs, long and searching, pierced her brain and left her addled.

That is her myth.

She has paranoid schizophrenia, and when she misses her medication (which helps only a little anyway), she wears an honest to goodness tin foil hat. I do not know when she stopped taking it this time. I hadn't been counting the pills like I should have.

Stute was ever hopeful, even clinched like that in the doorway. "Momma?" he said. He was black hair and black eyes and hope, not a bit of him matching either our mother or me. I knew his father, and I wonder how such a kind man could have left his baby boy with the two of us. How, as he'd fled our mother's madness, he hadn't taken the child, hadn't clutched the baby to his chest, shielded him from what he must have known the future held. But he did leave, taking nothing with him, disappearing before the crib was even put together.

"Momma?" Stute said again.

It's amazing how long you can stand by an open door and not look in. Hours, days, years. Ten-year-old Stute growing old as we stood there, my hand on his shoulder now, his voice tumbling around in that government-funded apartment, rolling around in our mother's silence. But he stepped forward and then my hand wasn't so much holding him as being held by his movement. He was pulling me. We were in. No turning back.

I looked around, and the tendons holding my jaw tightened. I had no idea that Saran Wrap came in colors—pink and blue and minty green, spring pastels. Mother had glued every hue to every wall, and she stood shaking in the center of her kaleidoscope, the covered windows streaming in cathedral colored light.

I didn't realize she was crying right away. Not until Stute was tangled around her, hugging her and whispering the same nothings I'd whispered to him when he was a baby, hungry and scared.

I think I said, "What?" Something useful like that.

She knotted her hands in our boy's curls; "I can't reach," she said. "I just can't do it."

My gaze followed hers. The ceiling was empty, normal. Patched and white, it was stained orange in places from water damage, a spider web crack pulling at the edges near the corner. Blessedly normal.

I wondered if finding her a ladder, stealing or borrowing one from the front office, would make our lives better or worse. I wondered how she'd bought so much Saran, so much paste, if she'd paid with the money I kept in a drawer in my room. I shook my head as Stute rubbed her stomach, his small gold hand tracing a moon into her belly.

"Essie. Essie, baby," she called to me.

But I stopped listening, leaving the two of them in that glimmery Easter egg, and walked to my room.

"Essie," she kept saying, "Essie, Essie," the climbing wail that was my name finally getting lost in the crackle of the Violent Femmes. The music beat its way out of the shell of a stereo I'd found on a curb while getting high with a boy who lived in the dorms at LSU. When I turned it up, the speaker got tinny and rattled and the sound never got loud enough for a neighbor to complain, never really satisfied that way, but I turned anyway, clicking the knob all the way around. Eventually, Stute followed me and curled himself up at the foot of my bed. I didn't bother trying to carry him to his own, even once his soft, baby snores mixed with the music.

She is right about Roosa. I looked him up. He was a smoke jumper and an astronaut and was the man who visited the moon with a pack full of seeds.

My myth:

I am a normal girl. I have a father, somewhere. I have a mother I will not have to commit. I will not have to go to the coroner's office and sign paperwork. I will not have to apologize when she bites the paramedics. I will not know that shock therapy is the therapy of last resort. I will not learn about the paralytic she will be given to stop her body from convulsing, from shaking itself apart. I will not know that she will sleep through it, may lose her memory, may become nauseous, may vomit, may hate me, may ache, may not get any better.

I will only know the things other girls know. What is on television tonight. What is at the movies. What dancing at prom feels like. I am normal. I am not a moon tree.

Of course, none of that is really true, either.

One of Roosa's moon trees was planted in New Orleans, right along the River Walk. A Loblolly Pine. Her trunk is rough, and when my friends climb into Cilia's Toyota to leave Baton Rouge behind, I always beg for a space so I can lay my hands against the Loblolly's scratchy surface while the others prowl the Quarter. Sometimes I sit there all night, drinking a forty out of a paper bag and wondering what it'd be like to disappear amongst the New Orleans homeless, the sourness of the Gulf washing over me, imagine myself baptized in the stink of it, holy there.

Once, a couple of years before Stute was born, my mother brought me to the aquarium, and after we watched the fish and had beignets, she took me to see the Loblolly. She never lowered her voice as she explained that we were sisters, me and this tree, that I was as hard inside as her trunk, which was good, I'd need it. I was probably about six at the time.

"It's the bark that will save you," she said, and I imagined that meant something and tried to find the hardness at my center, pressing my fingers into the soft flesh of my belly every night.

It wasn't long after the plastic wrap incident that our mother started breaking completely apart.

"Get out of my head, bitch," she screamed one night after I asked what she wanted for dinner. "Get your god-damned tendrils outta my brain."

Stute just watched her, big black eyes blinking.

I opened a can of ravioli, wondering what it would be like to eat brand name food, Chef Boyardee instead of Wal-Mart's Great Value. I was sick of her screaming, sick of working to feed us all, sick to death of her shit. "So, noodles?" I said.

I'd overheard her singing "Spaghetti is ready, baby, spaghetti is ready" to the mirror earlier that day and had decided to be cruel. Decided to make her think I was in fact reading her thoughts. I'd looked in the cabinet for SpaghettiOs, found only the ravioli. Close enough.

"Bitch!" She started sobbing.

I felt guilty then, but the truth was that it didn't matter what I said; she believed what she believed with or without evidence. I was a ghost to her, incorporeal, not really there at all.

"You like ravioli." I poured the can into a pot. "Stute, grab some bread." He pulled himself up off the floor where he'd been doing homework. The Saran Wrap was now on the carpet too, nailed and tacked and even stapled in spots. It stuck to his thighs as he moved. I watched her watch it shift and pull under him, watched her hands jump around, little nervous doves, as Stute left her floor disheveled, parts of the brown carpet showing through.

"Toast," I said to him, watching her carefully.

"I know what you two are doing," she said.

It was the first time she'd included Stute in her delusions, and I knew that he'd start coming to Pizza Hut with me weekend mornings. He could roll silverware while I waited tables.

"I don't think she wants ravioli," Stute said, the sweet of his voice like nothing I've ever had.

"But we do."

"Yes, we do," he said, grinning at the toaster, our mother's tantrum suddenly a million miles away.

That night, I shook him awake, laid a pair of blue swim trunks across his frame, and rubbed sleep from his cheeks. "The beast is down," was all I said.

Stute rarely asked questions, was the sort of kid that just watched everything. After dinner he'd watched our mother cut her hair in jagged strokes, and I'd watched him growing ever older under her shadow.

"Dress," I said.

He put on the too-large Goodwill trunks without a word, as if dressing for school or shopping, as if, even pulling on swimwear at midnight, we were normal.

"I want to show you something." I hoped he'd ask me what, but he didn't.

Mother was asleep on the couch, the empty bottle that helped her settle down nearby, as good as a teddy bear. She looked small, as if part of her body had lost itself in the scratchy plaid pillows. Stute and I each had our own rooms, and I always hoped her sleeping on the couch was an act of love and not paranoia, hoped she was being generous giving us the only bedrooms and wasn't just afraid of our rooms' small, dark corners.

The bottle of cheap vodka told us there was no need to tiptoe, and, anyway, silence was a lost cause with the stick of plastic popping with each step, so we moved quickly instead of quietly, each of us wearing nothing but used, ill-fitting bathing suits.

"Breathe deep, kiddo," I said once we were outside, and he rewarded me with a noisy swoosh of exhale. Car exhaust and jasmine, the smells of Baton Rouge, filled our lungs.

"Once upon a time," I said, pointing to the full, autumn moon. In Stute's story, we were both moon trees. I explained that we'd fallen to earth as something more than seeds, best friends, angels, had become separated in the atmosphere, grown legs instead of roots so we could always find each other.

I talked as we walked, Stute's hand sweating in mine.

He laughed at the idea of it all. "That's silly," he said, the lights of passing cars making his face less serious, more childlike. "If I'd been to the moon, I'd remember. I have an excellent memory, Ms. Becca says so."

"It's just a story," I said, sounding empty. I wondered what we looked like to the people on the road, decided we should cut through the neighborhoods where there'd be fewer cars. Mosquitoes swarmed us, and I wished I'd thought to spray him. "You sure like school, don't you?" I shook my head, my brother, so alien to me.

"It's good. I'm good at it." He'd skipped fifth grade and was making As in sixth. I, on the other hand, had dropped out about halfway through ninth grade. The notes my teachers sent home always said I wasn't living up to my potential, but nobody read them except me, and it was just easier one day not to go back, not to look at their disappointed faces, to get high in the park instead. Now, I made sure to read all of Stute's notes, to sign our mother's name for him. I wondered if he'd go to LSU one day.

"You can climb a tree, right?" We were almost there.

"I'm not a baby."

"Good." I pulled him into the sort-of woods that lined a nearby apartment complex, the scraggly trees planted in neat rows alongside the buildings making it seem more upscale than our own. "Around this way," I whispered. We hit a wooden fence, scrambled up a tree and then over it.

On the other side was a small swimming pool, the sort that was lit from within. A faded blue sunflower made of cracked tiles decorated the bottom. Stute clapped, and I imagined his toddler self, always laughing. And then his thin body was fracturing the water's surface, and as he rippled beneath it, I thought of crystal balls, the bright scarves of the fortunetellers in the Quarter, imagined I was seeing some future version of him tumbling about in the mist of precognition. A happy kid.

To escape the mosquitoes, I joined him. The water, warm as a bath, was still cooler than the night, and so I watched him swim, my head ducked under, holding my breath and ignoring the sting of chlorine. I wondered what it would take for us to live in a place like this, what it would take for Stute to swim all the time.

There was a tap on my head, and a cop stood looking down at me.

"Essie," he said.

When your mom is a schizophrenic and you're a truant, the local cops are rarely strangers. Stute swam on, oblivious. "Officer," I said back, unable to remember his name, embarrassed that he had mine.

"What are y'all doing here?"

I thought about saying "swimming" but had learned long ago not to be smart, that this cop was okay, sympathetic. He'd seen our mother at her worst, had even pulled her screeching off of the back of the man at the gas station when she decided that he was using the security cameras to watch her bathe, the two miles between the Circle K and the apartment an irrelevant fact.

I just shrugged.

He sat down on a nearby lawn chair, wiped the sweat off his face. "Come on out. Let's talk."

I decided to leave Stute flipping under the water. "How'd you know we were here?"

"Well, I didn't exactly know it was you two, but a guy called, said he saw a couple of kids in bathing suits skulking around nearby. It wasn't hard to figure where to look."

"I'm no kid," I said, wondering if he'd arrest us.

"How old are you, now?"

"Eighteen."

"Yeah." He sighed. "Get your brother. Y'all can't exactly stay here."

"Are we going to jail?"

He just shook his head. "Get Stuart." He moved his arm, the motion vague. "Come on, I ain't got all night."

He drove us home, sent Stute into the apartment and kept me in the car. "How bad?"

"It's fine. We're fine." I prayed he wouldn't come inside, wouldn't see.

He handed me a card. "Call if she gets... if you need anything. And remember, you have a record, your brother doesn't need one too." He smiled at me. "Stay the fuck out of trouble, okay?"

"Yeah." I had no pockets for the card, kept it tight in my hand. "Sorry about the seats," I said, looking at the puddles we'd left.

The thing about the Loblolly Pine on the River Walk is that without the plaque, you'd never know it was special. There really isn't anything astonishing about the moon trees. As a matter of fact, some of them are lost. No one bothered to keep track of where they'd been planted, had never even made the plaques. They grew at standard rates, were blown over by winds, were swallowed by forest fires, dropped acorns, held tree houses, got taller, wider, died.

They looked exactly like everything else.

Our mother was beautiful—when she showered, combed her hair.

She forgot to eat, or thought meals were poisoned, or just refused, and so stayed fashionably thin, looked lovely in a sundress, good light, made a good impression. People like pretty. Unless she was in a full-blown break, outsiders rarely saw the depth of her disease. At worst they thought she was odd, quirky, antisocial.

Sometimes, when the meds were just right, the rare Goldilocks cocktail leaving her not too hot, not too cold, she was the most fun you could imagine, making forts out of sheets and pillows. Covering the whole house with those forts, just for you. Letting you be the princess with a sword, a dragon killer, and then squealing right along with you as you chased her from fort to fort.

I think maybe it was like that sometimes. Mostly it wasn't.

So she screams a lot, strangers seemed to say, looking at us with slit eyes, but, hey, she wasn't so much a bad mother as one you wouldn't want, right? In all of our years of crazy, no one ever checked on us, and if they had, I would have told them everything was all right.

We were fine, normal, had no need for a plaque.

So I put the cop card away. Didn't even bother to read his name.

After ravioli night, she decided everything was rotten, or poisoned, or filled with mind control bugs. So I bought her Slim Fast shakes. The way they were sealed tight, the strangely thick walls of the cans, seemed to comfort her. The girls at my school had practically lived off them, so I figured she'd be fine, get her nutrients.

"Don't touch," she screamed as I unloaded a bag of groceries. We didn't have a car and lugging Slim Fast and peanut butter and canned soup in the heat had left me with a headache. I needed to escape.

"You unload the fucking bags then," I said, and she was crying again. Her blonde hair, so dirty it had begun to look brown, was matted in places. I imagined gathering her up and running a bath, telling her to close her eyes so I could soap her hair. I knew it would soothe her, the running water, the smell of Ivory soap, but instead I walked out of the apartment. Found a guy I knew, stayed away until dusk.

When I finally did go home, I could hear Stute crying as I opened the door, and the taste of bile suddenly mixed with the sweet spice of the cloves the boy'd smoked while we fucked. "Baby?"

Stute wasn't in the living room, but she was—just sort of wandering in the dark, the space too small for her to do more than pace a figure eight, and I suddenly thought of the rabid dog in *To Kill a Mockingbird*.

"Stute?"

I found him under my bed, hysterical and hiccupping, shaking so hard I wondered if it hurt. I checked his golden skin for marks, turning his arms, his legs, lifting his shirt, pulling and tugging so I could see every bit, as if that would absolve me.

"I'm sorry, I'm sorry," I said, too afraid to ask, and seeing blood on his foot, I began to shake too, finding his frequency, matching it. But there was no cut, and soon I was pulling myself free of him, running to the living room, flipping on lights.

The scissors were still in her hand, and I wondered how I could have missed them on the way in. They glinted so. "Mother?"

"Why do you all hate me?" she said, and when she turned I could see her face was bleeding, her arms, her hands, all bloody.

"No."

"I can't get you out, Essie." she said, shrugging. "I mean, I tried." She sounded so tired. "But, I can still feel you growing in me."

The wounds seemed small, as if she had been nipped and nipped by a rat, and I understood suddenly that I was a thing to be cut out, excised. That Stute had had to watch her with those scissors, had had to put his hands up to try and stop her.

"I'm sorry," I said moving toward her carefully, but the scissors were limp in her hand. She had given up.

I looked at Stute in the doorway. He was small for ten, had never grown right in our shadows.

I told him everything would be all right, told him to go borrow a neighbor's phone.

Later the cop helped with her paperwork.

When I was little, I would imagine that Roosa was my father, that my mother's story had some truth to it. I searched pictures of him for similarities, wondered if my hair was maybe a little red, if the size of my ears matched his.

There was no hidden message, though, no mysterious truths. No father there.

But I had that, that dream, that escape, that idea. I had Roosa. Stute just had me. And Momma.

When he was born, the doctors made sure she had antipsychotics pumping through her veins constantly, and she loved Stute so very much that she complied. She took the pills and held the baby. But she still wasn't good with being all there, and so I learned quickly to cradle his neck so his heavy head would not bounce, to test the heat of the formula on my wrist.

And he revolved around her, his little hands touching her always, opening and closing, so that I imagined he could catch her that way, that his grasping could keep her fluttering mind still, sane for both of us.

And when she would retreat, the copper flecks in his dark eyes would fall on me, and his little hands seemed to grow around mine, rooting me there with him.

The cop says that if she does not get better, if she does not *respond to the treatment*, it is unlikely the state will give me custody of Stute.

And I wonder if that would be better.

There are hundreds of moon trees.

Hundreds.

But the thing is, even though we lost some, once upon a time everybody wanted one.

Even the emperor of Japan adopted a moon tree.

They were that loved.

Shallowing

Karo swung the muzzle of the shotgun up and trained the barrel on a dove. From the doorway of the sagging porch, she could see several pairs in trees on both sides of the bayou, but she kept her focus tight. She didn't pull the trigger, she just sighted down the barrel, leading her target as it lifted into the air. After a while, she lowered the gun, a Remington 870 her father gave her nearly a year ago for her nineteenth birthday, picked out another dove, swung it up again, and keeping her back, neck, and head straight, she leveled the gun to her eye, not her eye to the gun. She watched the birds this way until her anxiety eased.

The doves were out of season, and Karo didn't hunt anyway. She liked sighting them, though. It made her feel good, doing something that came natural, easy. Something she could do in her sleep. No struggle, no thinking.

In the morning, she'd once again try to tell her father she was leaving college.

She pulled the gun back up. Trained it on a fat, red squirrel with a high tail. "Boom," she said, "Boom. Boom," as it crossed from branch to branch, pretending to shoot it over and over as it knocked paper-shell pecans to the ground.

When she dragged herself out of bed the next day, hung over from drinking on the porch after her father'd gone to bed but ready to come clean, he'd already left for work, a bouquet of swamp lilies he'd set out in a tin coffee can the closest thing to a note she'd get.

Charlie showed up at her window with a six pack around noon and badgered her to come out in the air with him. "You're only home for the summer," he said and she didn't tell him she was home for good.

That she didn't like Tulane. That New Orleans always smelled bad. That she was failing. Everything.

And she thought it was a date, finally a date, Charlie showing up like that. She told him to hold on and slipped into her suit and cut-offs as fast as she could. But they didn't make it two houses down the bank before meeting up with a few others, and the six pack became one of four and then one of six and when they got to the crick in the bayou where the bank swelled high enough to jump from, the dirt became crowded with discarded jeans and tank tops and faded blue work-shirts. A good fourth of her old high school class was there, basically just where she'd left them at Christmas, at Thanksgiving, last summer, the summer before that.

Someone stole a nylon rope off a nearby skiff and Karo tied a monkey's fist in the tail end before climbing the old twin oak, scraping her knee like a twelve-year-old and trying not to yelp. She fixed the other end to the farthest branch and shimmied back down the trunk, the nooks and juts and forks she put her hands and feet on as familiar as her own childhood bed.

She was the last to jump. Sunlight flashed off the water below so brightly that she had to squint whether she looked up or down. She took a running leap off the height of the bank, and then Karo was in the air, legs wheeling over the water, fingers clutched above the monkey's fist. The moment before letting go always filled her with tight panic, but now it was just more of the same stomach sick fear she'd worn for months. If she chickened out and held on too long, her hands burning from the effort, she'd hit the muddy water where it was shallowing. She knew the jutting bed below held shifting rocks and roots and branches that could crack her bones and scar her skin. She'd seen a boy break his leg here when she was thirteen, had helped pull him from the water, and now as she swung, the memory of his head lolling on the surface, eyes open way too wide, came to her.

The sweet spot was right after the lowest point in the rope's speeding arc, and Karo let go just as she wanted to grip the tightest. A catcall from the shore followed her down and she hoped it was Charlie.

Charlie whose hands found her stomach under her shirt the couple of times they'd kissed, bored or drunk or she didn't know what. Times she didn't know how or why they started or stopped.

Everyone else seemed to like the fall from the rope, sounding like drunks at a parade, hooting and hollering all the way to the splash. But she hated those seconds. Karo's favorite part, the only part worth anything at all, was there, right after she hit the water, exploding past the surface. It was in the silence after that initial shock, where gravity itself seemed to struggle, its pull fighting friction, her arms floating up as her torso plunged down.

That was where she wanted to live.

Something brushed past her leg, and Karo choked on silty brine. She'd tried to scream, sucked in water instead. She scissor kicked to the surface and sputtered there, her friends laughing from the bank. She didn't like this part of the bayou. Deep enough to hold their plunging bodies, it hid life, the water still and cloudy underneath you.

Last night, her father told her that he'd killed an alligator that had been hanging around their end of the bank. "Barely a week ago," he said. "It's been busy here," he said. He'd looked at her over his coffee, his hip leaned against the kitchen cabinet and had confessed to rolling the animal under a log after the last bend in their stretch of the bayou. Hiding it there to rot. The kill was out of season. "What do you do? The damn thing was a foot off our pier every morning. And the Wheeler baby has just started walking. You should see her—" he said. While he was hiding the carcass, she'd been asleep in her dorm. Skipping a final.

She slipped into a breaststroke and pulled as fast as she could, trying to beat whatever had slithered past. She was a good swimmer, a strong swimmer, and it only took a few strokes for her to feel safe, her toes bouncing at the riverbed as she struggled to stand and climb the bank.

Charlie put his arm in and caught her like he might grab a catfish, his hand sliding down her shoulder, past her bicep, towards her elbow as he searched for his grip and Karo could smell him, a smell faintly like turned over earth. "See," he said as if they'd made a bet and he'd won. As if she'd fought coming out to swing and swim with him. "See?"

"See what? I'm the one who climbed up and put out the rope," Karo said.

"But you didn't want to."

And Charlie was right. Karo did it because he'd asked.

She sat down on the towel she'd brought and leaned back into the heat. Hoped Charlie would sit with her. Instead, he took another run at the rope.

She didn't bother to watch. Knew he'd fly with grace, fall with grace, even sputter to the surface with grace. He was that sort. Karo covered her eyes with her hand and leaned all the way back so that her face pointed directly into the sun and her fingers glowed orange and she imagined the water lifting from her skin in a steam.

"City, you want another beer?"

Karo nodded. She didn't have to look to see who was talking or to know they were talking to her. She'd sat in class with each and every person there from first grade to twelfth—tenth or eleventh for those that dropped out. They lived in a two school bend in the road that no one moved to and barely anyone figured out how to move from.

And she was the only one they called City.

The other three or four who'd gone off to school, stayed gone. Karo just lacked their sense.

Charlie didn't sit next to her until she'd had two more beers and was ready to leave, but when he did, he dripped cool water across her legs and she forgot how hot and bored and tired of the noise she was. He put a hand around her ankle. "You coming out later?"

At Tulane "out" meant a bar filled with smoke on a street that smelled like piss. Here it meant a field or a clearing, usually not far from the smell of manure or swamp gas. Or it had when they were in school together. "You going to tip cows?"

"That's some ignorant shit."

She made a show of rolling her eyes at her own failed joke, one that people at Tulane used on her when she told them where she was form, trying to be too cool for any of it. But she wanted to go where Charlie went. "Yeah, probably." She'd meant to have dinner with her daddy tonight. Maybe finally come clean. But Charlie's hand was on her. "Yeah," she said, again, putting her fingers back over her eyes and collapsing to the towel like she could hardly feel his fingers tight against her ankle, biting at her there.

Karo took the laundry basket from her father. Told him to sit, let her be useful.

"I don't know why you can't date a boy in New Orleans," he said. He poured them both a long shot of whiskey and then moved aside the can of lilies. He waited to sip from his glass until Karo put the basket down on the kitchen counter where the flowers had been. "Charlie is, at his goddamn best, a pain in the ass," he said.

"He's cute." Karo didn't tell her father that she was mostly invisible to the men in her classes at Tulane. Or how badly things went when she wasn't. How she drank and fumbled, a failure at dating. How she'd apologize by putting her hands on them. How she'd beg by wrapping her legs around their hips. How they left her feeling disheveled and bruised. Instead, she folded a worn bath towel. "And I've crushed on him since tenth grade. Hangers?"

Her father pointed back to the laundry room. It was the size of a closet. "Still in the top cabinet. He thinks he's already a game warden. Gave Bunky shit the other day for baiting. Poor guy ain't hurting anybody. He can barely walk, his back gotten so bad. He certainly can't stalk a deer."

Karo didn't know anything about Charlie being a game warden or wanting to.

"It's hilarious. I mean Bunky ain't no saint, for sure, but he ain't poaching. That's private land." He put his glass down, took the towel she'd just folded, opened it, and refolded it—his way. "Your boy is just being a pain in the ass. No, don't do that. You're stretching the elastic all out. Give me those."

Karo handed him the socks she'd just rolled and then took a pull from her glass. She tried to remember the last time she'd spoken to a game warden. They were always old guys, weren't they? Ex-cops? "Isn't he too young?" The ones she'd had run-ins with were all the sort that liked to mess with high school kids who were drinking their parent's beer in pontoon boats, not bothering anybody.

"I'd expect he'll have to finish some sort of degree over at the Tech School, but he's not exactly a kid. He's a year older than you." Her father edged her out of the way and pulled another towel from the basket. "And look at you. Killing them over in New Orleans." He said every syllable, drawing them out so it sounded like New Oar-leans instead of the one syllable word her classmates used: N'awlins. "Go grab me those hangers, huh? And let me deal with my own damn laundry. You're messing this all up."

Karo put her hands out in defeat and slipped behind him to go for the hangers. Charlie had barely finished high school. Had spent the last three years getting drunk and sponging off his parents. He was a fuck-up. A wonderful fuck-up. He was not a guy with a plan or a future. He just wasn't that sort.

She was that sort. She always had been.

The grade report she'd printed out for her father was on the fridge, under the same chipped magnet he'd used to hold up her report cards when she was in elementary school, a faded clay raccoon mooning the kitchen, the words "Coon-Ass" across its very human butt cheeks. The printout said what it was supposed to say, that she'd made As in all her classes last semester. Just like she always did. That she'd taken calculus and chemistry. That she was a star, an engineering major with a bright future. She'd laid it out herself in Excel, after all.

A good forgery job.

Her glass was empty and the whiskey was next to her father, so Karo just stood there wanting a drink and hoping he wouldn't turn around and catch her, red faced and shaking.

When Charlie stopped by the next day, she was on the porch sighting a turkey vulture circling the woods on the far bank.

"Not very good eating," he said, causing her to jump.

"Jesus. I'm holding a goddamn gun."

"I didn't exactly sneak up."

Karo leaned the shotgun against the railing. "Daddy says you're in school."

He stepped onto the porch, flooded with early sunlight, and sat in her father's sliding rocker, pulled the bill of his baseball cap down. "Just a class. Introduction to Forest Technology. I'm taking it online, but some things are hands on. There was a whooping crane count last week." He drummed his fingers on the wood of the chair, making a flat tune. "I didn't actually see any. They released fourteen this year. I think our population is up to twenty-nine now. It would be a thing to see one, wouldn't it?"

She knew that even of those released cranes that survived, some would relocate, migrate to better nesting grounds. She nodded. "A thing."

"Why didn't you come out last night?"

Karo picked the gun back up. Cited the vulture again. "You want to know a secret?" she said.

"Sure."

Another vulture crossed in front of the one she was watching. What she wanted to say was, "I'm flunking out of school and I mismanaged my money and so can't afford food, much less the apartment I share with a woman who hates me." Instead she said, "There's a dead alligator under the far, far log on the right over there. Way down."

"You mean under the vultures? Did you see it?"

Whatever the birds were circling, it was on land and a good fifty feet from the log her father had showed her from their jon boat, but she nodded anyway. Then she said, "I didn't see it. I just heard some kids talking." For a moment, she'd thought taking Charlie to the carcass would be like a gift. The sort of thing he'd be interested in. It'd give them something more to talk about, an excuse to go out on the water alone together.

"Not much of a secret, then," he said and she felt stupid. "Want to come and swim? Everyone is over by the bridge." He must have pulled out of the chair, because he nudged her arm. "We're going to have a fish fry. Do it up right."

Karo stood very still, but his hand flitted away as quickly as it had landed. "Maybe in a little while," she said. Her house was between his and the bridge. She was a rest stop. She breathed in deep, trying to catch his smell, but he wasn't standing close enough. She sighted the turkey vulture again. "You really going to be a fish cop?" It came out angry somehow.

"Better than ending up a burnout river rat," he said.

She didn't answer and after a few moments of silence, Charlie left. She dropped the barrel and watched him walk across the yard, wondering if he knew. Then she raised it, found the brown of his sandals and followed them up the bank with the Remington. "Boom," she said, "Boom. Boom."

The garage where her father worked on big engines was not really normal walking distance from the house. There were no sidewalks between them, just gravel roads, catfish ponds, and milo fields, but Karo set out anyway, a bottle of Gatorade and a sandwich in the backpack she'd brought home from school. After half an hour, she was drenched in sweat. She sat on the edge of a ditch and pulled out her lunch, the clutch of pines behind her offering no shade, but she didn't want to move into the dark space between them. In the heat of the day, it looked like a cool haven for rattlesnakes.

It took another half hour to get there and the bottle of Gatorade was long gone when she did. Before she found her father, she slipped into the bathroom and drank directly from the dirty sink, her head wedged between the drain and the spigot. Despite her deep tan, her arms and cheeks were pink and painful. Another stupid decision. She tried to dry the sweat from her body as best she could, but her shirt clung to her with it and her hair was soaked and matted.

When she found him, her father was bent over a large, rusted tractor, his blue coveralls smeared with grease and sweat stains. She tried to watch him without saying anything, to just sit back and see him, but when she stepped in front of the box fan for a little relief, he must have felt the change in air. He looked up. "Good lord, girl. What are you doing here?" He squinted. "Did you walk here? Is something wrong?"

Dirt was smudged deep into the cracks around his eyes and mouth. He looked old. Karo was suddenly aware that she wasn't exactly sure of his age. Her own father.

"Karo?"

She wondered how much he made. A scholarship covered some of her tuition. And she'd taken out loans. But he paid her cell phone bill. Her electric bill. Bought her a laptop for Christmas. Sent her spending money. The wrench in his hand looked huge. A heavy thing.

"Nothing. No," she said.

"You look—" He stepped up to her, the wrench in his hand still, and she thought of a lie she'd told a man she'd met online, that her father was an accountant. A silly, stupid thing. "Are you okay?" he said.

"Just hot."

He made her sit at the workbench and brought her a Coke from the vending machine. Wetted down a thick, blue paper towel and pressed it to her head, the back of her neck. "You're not nauseous, are you?" he said, checking for symptoms of heat stroke.

She stayed the rest of the afternoon watching him from the workbench. Watching other mechanics come and go. Watching the light from the open bay shift around him as he worked. When he bloodied his knuckles under the hood of a John Deere, he wouldn't let her bandage him. "Sit," he said, whenever she tried to help. "Sit, sit."

And so she sat, the warble of the box fan keeping time as her father moved around the garage. He was a bear of a man, ungraceful but strong, competent. His pace was slow, but he didn't lumber. Still, as he wrestled the metal bones from a combine, heaving with his legs bent low, she wondered if he was slower than the last time she'd spent an afternoon watching him work, and then realized she never had, the times she'd come here before, all those afternoons, she'd colored, played with a wrench like a doll, then as she got older, done homework, read books, flirted with the young guys who apprenticed there. She'd never really bothered to sit still and just watch him. Not at work. Not at home.

The next day, Karo waited on the porch for Charlie to stop by, ask her to join him somewhere. When he finally came, he was part of a group, cutting across the yard to get back to the deepest part of the bayou. "Swim?" he hollered.

She followed them a few steps behind, hoping Charlie would fall back and talk to her, and when he didn't, she broke off from the group completely and wandered the bank alone, finally doubling back to the house.

She poured whiskey into a coffee mug and sat on the floor in the kitchen to drink it. She'd stopped promising herself that she'd tell her father tonight, in the morning, tomorrow. That Charlie would fall in love with her. That everything would be okay.

What she wanted was to run away.

She pulled the Remington from the mahogany cabinet where it stood with the other guns. All of them, even the antiques, had been used to hunt. As always, she put some birdshot into her pocket, just in case, and made a mental note that it would be a nice surprise for her father if she cleaned all the guns, dusted the cabinet when she got back.

The jon boat was already in the water, its flat hull gently rocking against the pier. From it, she sighted egrets and squirrels and a blue heron that lifted a water moccasin from the bank. She motored in short bursts along the waterway, drifting just to watch the world go by in between them.

Eventually she pulled onto the bank of a little swamp island, a clutch of cypress trees that trapped enough dirt to be a real stretch of land. She'd decided to camp there, to spend a night away from everyone, from herself. She pulled the boat onto land and tied it off, just in case the water climbed the bank higher than she expected. The whine of cicadas and mosquitos ramped up around her until it was a long buzz that made her think of rattlesnakes, and she loaded the shotgun.

Under the back bench of the jon boat, there was a waterproof sack that held a tarp, a notebook and pen, her father's fishing license, and a flask. The flask was empty. She'd put a block of cheese and a Gatorade into her backpack before leaving and she made a little picnic, smoothing the tarp under the branches of a cypress and sitting there, watching the sun settle onto the water, dipping past by the time she'd finished the cheese.

She opened her father's notebook and flipped through it in the dying light. There was little there. Gas prices. Fishing notes. She read every page, hoping to find him in the neat, small handwriting.

A rustle in the brush near the bank made her draw the gun up, but a flash of white told her it was a crane, and she held the barrel steady. Sighting.

Her father had told her, "There are better places than this," when she was younger. "A whole damn world." And she'd believed him. Reached out to it. Thought she belonged in it.

She made a clucking sound and the bird burst out of the brush. It was huge, a snowy giant with black tipped wings that it beat against the air before taking off. Charlie's whooping crane.

She trained the barrel on it, leading the target just as her father'd taught her when she was a child. When they would hunt for dinner and then make it together. When she was a part of his life here.

"Boom," she said, pretending to shoot, her finger hovering above the trigger, "Boom. Boom." The bird flapped its great wingspan, the motion fluid now that it was airborne, and lifted ever higher, a twig falling from its grip and spinning toward Karo's little bit of earth.

She squeezed the trigger. A deliberate motion.

The bird crumpled, a bit of red on its breast, an unnatural bend in its left wing. It beat the other one harder and harder, wrestling against its own weight, gravity, the growing red in its chest as it plunged to the ground. Karo could hear it, struggling there. Dying there. But she stayed on the tarp, the tense pain in her stomach easing only after it completely stilled.

Pulpo

Her papa's hands tremble as he opens the olives—something she can do but asks for help with, anyway. It is the same sort of lid the octopus she is studying in her lab opens to dig for shrimp while she clicks the buttons on her stopwatch. In a race, Papa would shake into second, the octopus leaving him far behind. Slow to leave the table where he chops this morning's catch, slow to take the jar, slow and fumbling as he turns the lid.

But fast enough to have caught them dinner: the *pulpo* from the first cast of the day, another octopus, but in his nets, in this house, on his tongue that still struggles with English, it is always "pulpo."

Tomorrow, she will feed *her* octopus scraps from his fishing nets, and its time will be shorter. It is a fast learner.

Her hand in a loose fist, she presses her thumb against an imaginary button, counts, pushes again. Slower. Her father is getting slower, as if every second gained in the lab is lost here at home.

She stays at work too long, wants to be back now. The octopus is amazing, learning as fast as Papa forgets. Its spots grow familiar, like a face. A friend.

She is not lonely there, at work.

She waits for the sound of the *pulpo* hitting oil, waits for the smell. Feels Papa's hand swim across her shoulder as he maneuvers around her.

The smell is the same as it has always been. Olive oil, garlic, the tart of a lemon cut, cut again. The salt and brine on his clothes, in the curtains, the smell of fish from his nets, her necropsies settled deep in the wood.

The house will remember even if they both forget.

She steals an olive from his cutting board, like a second from the stopwatch, and then a slice of *pulpo*, sizzling, from the pan. He pops her knuckles, wags his father finger with a smile: "Wait."

Still fast enough for that, too.

Deformed

Milas did not fully believe in God, but his grandmother had been born with a veil, a wet, milky membrane lying between her and her first breath like a thin sheet of the afterlife hooded over her face, and it, she insisted, had been *His* shrouded touch. The women of the neighborhood, keeping their fingers on their crosses and their voices slung low, said the veil gave her *the gift,* and they were not so very certain it was from *Him.* She could see and talk to ghosts. And despite the edge to their whispers, they all came. The aunts and cousins. The church ladies. The neighborhood hens. They would all visit constantly, each and every one of them asking for *messages.* They would come with pies or garden vegetables or empty, wringing hands, desperate to hear something from husbands, fathers, and sons dead too young, some lost to trucking and farming and oil field accidents, others eaten up with cancer, or drinking, or drugs, and a few, a few, sad men gone from just being shotgun tired of being tired and poor.

His own father, a rarely seen white man whose family tried to farm soybeans across the levee, had died after taking a bullet to the belly while buying drugs in town. Supposedly, even he had whispered a message to the old woman, but Milas told her to keep it to herself. He figured there was no need to talk to a dead man who'd found him too dark to talk to in life.

So Milas knew all about messages.

He was alone in the soup aisle of the Piggly Wiggly when he got his. The voice was worn and crackled, a woman's voice, soft around the edges like washed paper, like a receipt left in your pocket on laundry day.

"Boy, you going to make God cry," it said, then a series of clacks, a mouth snapping shut, strong teeth, a fierce tap, tapping.

Milas inched his hand away from the ramen on the shelf, shifted his feet. He was small and skinny, a runt of a man, with rough skin and hair just beginning to go grey and wiry. He stood there stooped, born with an old man's back, with his hand sort of paused in the air, and just listened.

The Piggly Wiggly was quiet, mostly deserted so late on a Monday. He could hear "Let it Be" slipping out of the speakers, but that was it. He looked across the floor, expecting to see old woman church shoes, but he was alone. He shook his head. The clacks seemed to echo in there, rolling around in his ears in much the same way he'd play his words across his teeth before he spoke.

He thought of his grandmother's dentures, ill-fitting and noisy. Thought of that bleached gator skull he'd found as a boy, its sharp, yellow teeth. Thought of summer Sundays with his aunt, the clack, clack of her fat hand slapping at his thigh as everyone else sang, "Glory Be."

Thought of church. Of things he'd done, not done.

He listened hard for breathing or shuffling, cocking his head to catch any noise that might leak through the rows of stacked Campbell's soup cans. Heard nothing.

Listened harder. Nothing.

Milas looked at his sandals, his knobby brown toes, and considered the silence. He rolled his left ankle, turning the foot inward and inward until he was met with a comforting pain. As a child, he'd become convinced that when people saw him, they saw deformities that did not exist in his own mirror, maybe seamed fingers, curled like crab claws, or a pocked face—leper-like, maybe a clubbed foot. For years, he'd found the idea soothing, a simple explanation for his loneliness. So now, waiting for something to happen, he pushed at his ankle until his foot looked small and curved—matching its angle to the sad pictures he'd seen on the internet—and thought about the voice.

He rolled the words around, whispered them to himself—"You going to make God cry."

A message.

Milas stepped away from his basket, ramen noodles and other essentials forgotten, and moved around the store, glancing down aisles. He passed the manager and a couple of stockers. No one smiled or waved despite the fact that he visited the store weekly and had gone to school with both of the men filling the shelves.

He walked slowly, unsure of what to do, found himself near the front of the store. The cashier, Katie, a second or third cousin on his mother's side, seemed to close her big brown eyes as he neared, and he imagined her revulsion. *Deformed.*

Then another voice caught him, this one a man's. Loud.

"Faggot."

He was used to being called things, but that was new, a curiosity. He turned a little, resting his hand against a nearby shelf, and there was Jeffrey Cole, shoulders stiff and squared in the way you'd see a bulldog do before a fight, puffing and straining. He was a mean son-of-a-bitch, from a family of mean sons-a-bitches. "Klan," his grandmother would say when she saw the Cole boys out, snapping her head in a little knowing nod, her mouth clamped and pursed so she swallowed the n. It wasn't a word he'd heard often, despite growing up in a small Louisiana town, so when he heard it, he knew it was real, not a rumor, and stayed clear.

Like the other men in his family, Cole'd been in and out of the parish jail his whole life and was certainly bound for Angola prison one day. He bloodied Milas's nose more than once when they were teens and still liked to call him *half-breed nigger* when he saw Milas walking to Dr. Breaux's where he did the books. The two of them past thirty now and Cole still hollering and throwing Budweiser cans at Milas from his dinged-up Vette as if they'd never graduated to adulthood.

But he wasn't looking at Milas now, he was looking past him. The man who had Cole's eye was near the baked goods, maybe five aisles down. He was white and tall, six foot something and soft around the middle, wore plastic framed glasses. He watched Cole, not moving, just looking at the wiry drunk, his face stuck in a half frown. The man looked confused more than angry, as if unsure what the word meant, maybe unsure if it was meant for him.

Then Cole was stepping forward, Milas almost missing the movement, only registering it as the stranger turned his back, refused the bait. He shoved past Milas, smelling like a bender. Walked quicker. And Milas knew that the man's back had been an insult, impossible to ignore.

"I'm talking to you, faggot," Cole growled. "Seen you last night, *faggot*," the word getting sharper each time he said it. "At the bar."

Milas could see both of the men, was a corner in their quickly shrinking triangle, and it seemed he could see their futures from where he stood. He knew that every man he grew up with had a knife in his pocket. He knew that Cole used his for more than scraping at his fingernails and prying things open.

"Listen to me." Cole had started to shout. "Don't need your kind around our kids." His face was all twisted up. "No faggot teaching my boy."

He was past Milas now, the soft stranger turning again at the sound of him, and Milas saw Cole's hard, thin shoulders pulling downward, no longer posturing uselessly, but drawing in, coiling strength, his hands near his pockets, his right hand *in* his pocket, his chin tucking into his neck—the rush about to come, and then Milas was grabbing something.

The shelf was short and loose, an endcap display, and it came off easily, Halloween candy and stuffed toys bouncing to the ground. The edges were sharp and dug into his hands, the small pain a comfort as Milas moved forward, as he swung, as the noise of the shelf hitting the back of Cole's head and neck swept over him, a sickening clack.

Then Cole was turning, too mean to fall, and Milas was swinging over and over and over, Cole on the ground now and Milas still swinging, slamming the metal shelf so the shudder running through it hurt his arms.

People were yelling.

Milas opened his eyes, unsure of when he'd closed them. He looked up at the stranger. The man's mouth was slack. "I..." Milas said, no other words coming to him.

Still holding the shelf, he backed up, not looking at Cole, only at the stranger. He could hear the store's fluorescent lights buzzing and a soft wet sucking sound at his feet, *Cole breathing*. Behind him, Milas thought he heard the ragged sound of someone crying. The world smelt burnt.

The stranger's head moved a little, a small no, and Milas turned and ran like hell, the clang of the shelf as it fell to the floor chasing him out the store.

He knew it would not take long for the police to find him at his grandmother's, but he went there anyway. His mother had taken him to the little wooden frame house when he was three. Then she left "to get her hair done, to see some friends" and had not come back. Every few years, she'd show up for two or three hours, and when she left, some trinket worth a couple of dollars would disappear with her. A broach his grandmother wore to church. A teapot she'd bought at the flea market. Even one of his games once, Street Fighter. "Drugs," his grandmother would say, patting his knee. He'd lived with the old woman from the day his mother left him until he was twenty, when he moved into an apartment of his own. But he stayed close, visiting every Sunday the fifteen years since, keeping her company when she got home from church.

He realized that everyone in the small town probably knew he'd go there before even he did, but, having no car, he'd run blindly, feet slamming the road, the grass, the railroad tracks, her porch. She'd died only a month ago, and the place would belong to the bank soon enough. Milas figured he might not get to see it again once they arrested him.

He moved into her bedroom and sat on the right side of the bed where he used to watch television with her after she got sick. The air was musty and sweet, her old woman smell still there in the corners. When he was about ten, she'd made the quilt on the bed from scraps she found in sale bins and flea markets, washing it until the scratch of cheap fabric had worn down, and the once garish blues, greens, oranges, and pinks had muted, fading prettily. He thought of her body under it in those last days, her skin more yellow than brown at the end, the quilt damp from her fevers. He thought of the way she'd pat his hand in time to the theme songs of the game shows they'd watch, and he pulled the blanket around his chest and started to cry.

"Boy," she'd say as she got sicker, rarely using the name her daughter'd given him, "ain't no good reason to live like this."

And he'd nod. *There really isn't,* he'd think, watching the window instead of her shows, the sound of her struggling to breathe filling him up.

She had taught him to be good, whipping him with a willow switch when he hit a cousin or talked back, had put him on the school bus and tried to make him go to church, had even paid for correspondence college courses—an accelerated program the high school offered gifted students—even though they both knew he'd never be able to afford to go off to school. She had educated him, kept him from drugs and from the wrong sort of crowd, and had believed that the strange, quiet child she'd been left with was, at least, good enough.

She would not recognize the man with the shelf.

There was a knock at her door, a soft tapping.

He waited, but no one burst through, no cops yelled, "Hands on your head." No search dogs growled and barked, just another quiet knock.

He pulled himself up after the third one, not bothering to wipe his wet cheeks.

The man knocking was the stranger from the store. He was not ugly, but the large plastic frames of his glasses fit poorly, making what could have been a pleasant face overly pale and small. Even softer, doughier close up, he was not quite fat, but moving in that direction. Across the street, barely visible in the blue black of the evening, one of the women from his grandmother's church watched them from her porch rocker, and Milas wondered what she would tell the neighborhood hens.

Without saying anything, he opened the door wider and stepped aside, letting the cool fall wind fill the room. The man looked in, tilting his head forward but otherwise not moving. Unsure of what to do, Milas shrugged and walked to the couch, rubbing his face down as he settled into the worn cushions. He twisted his foot sideways into the floor until a pain settled there, and only then did he speak. "I'm not like that, what I did there," he said softly, his hands covering his eyes.

The man said nothing, but after a while, Milas heard the door shut and felt the weight of the stranger settle next to him. He did not look up.

"Your cousin said I could find you here."

Milas said nothing.

"Honestly, I'm not sure why," the man hesitated and Milas focused on the soft whistle of his breathing, "why I wanted to."

Milas thought about that. "Is he dead?' he asked.

"No."

He moved his hands to his knees but kept his gaze down. "Good."

"Badly hurt, maybe."

Milas nodded, and they sat in silence. Finally, he turned to the man, "Why are you here?" Wondering why it was not the police who had come.

"Your cousin said you might have saved my life, somehow. Said that that man—"

"Jeffery Cole."

"That he was dangerous. Bad."

"We were in school together." Milas stood. "He carries a knife." He knew the words sounded weak, his own horrible violence so unimaginable that even Cole with a knife would seem sane in comparison. He understood now that his deformity was much deeper than he'd thought, that his soul was the bit that was twisted, grotesque. The birth defect deep inside him.

The man nodded a little. It seemed to take effort.

Again there was silence, and Milas itched to fill it. "I heard a voice, earlier today," he said, looking the man in the eye. "A message or a warning, maybe."

The man shifted his weight. "I told the officer that I didn't feel well. I told him I'd be in later to make my statement," he paused, his hands playing with a loose thread in the cushion. "They seemed in no hurry, like they had other places to be."

Milas wondered if the man had heard him. "The voice—"

"I thought I'd meet you first, before I said anything."

Then Milas got it. The man did not want him to be deformed and damaged. He wanted a happy ending. "You tell them what you saw. You tell them the truth. Everyone else will have, anyway."

The man nodded again. Then his head paused, his glasses tilting downward, sliding a bit against his nose. Milas looked down, following that tilt. His feet, his sandals, even the ends of his jeans were splattered with small dark red and burnt brown patches. Confused, he rubbed a foot against the spots on his leg. Then he understood. He held in a gag and stomach acid burned at his throat.

"It's an ugly word, what he called me, full of hate," the man said, not looking away from where Cole's blood had stained Milas. "In New Orleans, you hear it less, I think." He shook his head. "We moved here when my partner's mother got ill. It's different."

Milas tried to understand what he was supposed to say. It seemed the longest conversation of his life, maybe was.

"The rules are different here. Small town rules, I guess? Maybe we shouldn't have gone to the bar."

Milas shook his head. "I don't know."

"No." The man finally pulled his gaze away from the blood. "What did your voice tell you?"

He rolled the answer around in his mouth before saying it, "That I would make God cry."

The man nodded a last time, stood. He crossed to the door. "My mother said much the same thing to me when I told her I was gay," he said as he left the house.

Milas looked at the closed door. It was the same as it had always been, a simple, soft grey Cypress door, a long crack running through it. He wanted to go over to the door, to open it and check if the visit had been real, if the man was out there, walking to a car parked nearby. He wanted to turn the knob and say something better than what he'd said.

Instead he stood there, listening to nothing at all, and imagined telling a mother this thing, that you were gay, imagined the man finding his words, what that would be like, imagined telling a mother anything, that you were lonely, that you'd almost beaten a man to death, that you were deformed. He couldn't, his own mother a non-entity, and so he searched for his grandmother instead, wandering the house in ever tightening circles, the place too small with only four rooms.

Finally, he opened the kitchen door. It led to a small side yard where his grandmother had strung a clothesline and planted camellias. It was mostly a patch of concrete, the rectangle of dying grass a mere nod to the idea of a yard. A plastic lawn chair, missing straps and sun bleached to the color of fresh eggshells, stood at an angle near the door. It was tilted just right, so the seat caught the afternoon sun and the headrest stayed in the shade of the roof's overhang. A planter nearby had been turned into an ashtray and was filled with sand and the aging butts of Virginia Slims. His grandmother may have been Baptist, but she'd come out here for a pony of Miller and a smoke most afternoons, talking to a neighbor across the fence and resting her feet in the sun.

When he was old enough, he'd hung the wash while she visited, filling summer days doing small chores and eavesdropping on the business of old women. When he was too old, she'd chastise him, "Boy, you need to be chasing girls and getting out, as old as you are, not bothering these women." Then she would laugh gently, swatting at him.

Her camellias were fall bloomers, so their petals, pink and red, were just folding open, the flowers still tight enough to resemble fat roses. They were her favorites, and he'd continued to come once a week and water them even after he buried her.

He settled into her chair to watch the lightning bugs flash yellow and green in front of the petals. Milas tried to feel her there, to will her into talking. He thought of the voice in the grocery store. His grandmother had been fun, frequently laughing, a sociable woman who hated that her grandson had no friends. "It's enough to make an angel weep," she'd said often, making a fuss and praying loudly for him while clutching her white leather Bible in a tight fist. And when he was bad, she'd invoke the tears of God himself, as she beat him with her switch.

He thought of the sting of it, the green wood slapping at his thighs, her disappointment never soft, and then he thought of what he'd done, the feel of the shelf in his hands, the sound of the metal connecting with Cole's skull. He thought of the moment of pleasure when the other man had gone down. The sweet tightening in his gut, the lightheadedness.

The incredible need to swing again.

He slept a little, on and off, waiting for the sound of her voice, fighting sleep as hard as he could so that he'd wake suddenly, feeling sad and guilty. The lightning bugs' pulse a soft admonishment in the dark.

There was a beating on the door, loud enough that he heard it from the patio. The police. He didn't move. It seemed easiest to stay there. To wait with his grandmother's things.

The wind picked up and pulled at the camellias, whipping the branches left and right until even some of the tightest petals yanked free, dotting the concrete in red and pink. The banging got louder, and a cool rain started. He watched the fallen petals soak through, thought of his grandmother sweating under that quilt on her last night, thought of the brown spots on his jeans. Wet and tired, he ignored the banging. Just sat there, watching the flowers turn translucent under the porch light, sticking wetly to the concrete, the splotches soft around the edges like watercolors.

He tried to pray, but he did not want God, just her.

Clown

Taking acid from the bus boy had been a dumb idea. That was last night after close, when she was loopy and tired and flush with tips. Now Stacy was hiding in the Pizza Hut bathroom, her shift not ending for another hour. She leaned against the cool of the mirror. Her head hurt. Bad. She tried not to think about the people who went in and out of the Hut's bathrooms, their nasty hands touching everything. The cool just felt too good to move. The bus boy's acid had been dirty stuff, and when the fun of the drug wore off, Stacy tried to sleep but jitter-jangled instead. "Shit's cut with rat poison," Sal told her, "S'what keeps you up, makes you shake." Stacy didn't know if it was true, but she sure as hell hadn't slept.

And she felt dumber than shit.

A few weeks ago, Sal tried to make putting her on Kid's Night sound like it was a big a favor, handing her the clown suit and saying, "An easy gig, much less work than waiting tables. All you do is color with them," and, "You're artistic. You like kids."

But there were no tips, just lousy minimum, and since she wasn't moving around a lot, the night dragged. She'd never been much, maybe. Not even a real, honest to god, starving artist, like she told people. But Christ. She was wearing what amounted to a baby's onesie, the clown suit splattered in polka-dots from ankle to neck. A grown fucking woman. Her parents must be so proud. She pushed her knuckles into her thigh and tried not to cry.

The worst of it was that she really had to go. But she couldn't figure out how to get the damn clown suit off, what with her hands shaking so bad and the zipper down the back impossible to reach. She couldn't even manage to undress herself. She thought of the girl who used to wear the onesie, the quitter. "Ran off to greener fucking pastures," Sal told her. "Brighter than me," Stacy answered. And now, straining her arm to reach the zipper and finally giving up and deciding she'd just have to go later, she knew it was true: everyone was brighter than her.

She hated being the clown.

Careful not to look at her reflection, and went back into the dining room. The jukebox was playing "Baby Got Back." One of the kids had abandoned the coloring table and was performing on the small platform around the buffet. There were only a few diners in the place, but every last one of them watched the five-year-old in the little yellow dress put her chubby hands on the floor next to some stray tomatoes from the salad bar. All of them eating it up as she shoved her tiny butt high into the air, waggling it, the little Hello Kitties on her white cotton panties bouncing up and down to the beat.

People actually "awwwed."

Stacy tried to remember who the girl's parents were. Even though it was a relatively slow night, she wasn't sure, never really looked at customers' faces. Maybe that couple with the empties, laughing and smug. Yeah, the woman gave the kid a little wave. Her dye job almost matched the kid's sweet curls, the same basic blonde but harsher, brassier, like she was trying to dye herself young.

"Asshats," Stacy said, and a man in a nearby booth looked up.

She winked at him. It didn't really matter if he told the manager. Most nights, after they counted the till, she let Sal bend her over a flat of lettuce in the cooler, his hands warm on her shoulders. It wasn't likely she'd get fired anytime soon. She'd been screwing Sal for about two months, and if you ignored the clown thing, it had gone pretty well for her—choice shifts and free pulls at the beer tap.

Not that that was why she was doing him, but still. Sal was nice to her, even on the worst nights, always smiling at her when he touched her hair.

She looked at the kid. "Come on, munchkin. Time to color." She was a beautiful child, blue eyed and rosy, the fullness of her cheeks a stark contrast to the thin sullen kid in Stacy's own baby pictures.

"Time to dance!" the girl said, her butt still high in the air.

Stacy thought of her mother, a property lawyer who always looked smart in knee-length skirts. Trying on her mom's voice, all quiet and firm, she said, "That's not very lady-like."

The kid added a little hop to the booty shake, and her yellow dress flew completely over her head, the edges of it like little fluttering wings shifting around her ears.

This new dance was apparently hilarious. Everyone except Stacy laughing.

"Jesus, kid," she said, reaching her hand out. She was just trying to straighten the kid's dress, maybe straighten the kid, but the girl pulled away and fell off the platform. She looked, to Stacy, still tripping a bit from last night, like a stop motion cartoon, her fall quick and jerky, arms whirling, bright colors trailing behind the fluttering dress.

The girl hit her head on the tile floor.

After the crack, god, what a crack, there was nothing. Complete, clear silence as if even the air conditioner was too shocked to whir. Then the restaurant exploded—the kid squalling, everyone yelling, the parents rushing over from the table with the empties, the mom, Dye-Job, already screeching her head off.

Before the woman even checked on her daughter, before Stacy could apologize, before she could say anything at all, Dye Job's hands were in her face, her bright blue nails sliding past Stacy's eyes as she grabbed a chunk of her hair. Stacy yanked back, and stared at the clump of her own black strands in the woman's left hand, the smudge of white grease paint across her knuckles. Then the woman's fist popped out in a wild punch, slamming into Stacy's throat and sending her ass over tits.

Now Dye-Job stood there, screaming and ignoring her downed child. Stacy couldn't say anything, though, only cough and gasp, the bitter smells of Clorox and lemon floor cleaner falling across her tongue.

Everything moved in a tilted slide show then, no one helping her up for a while, and Stacy so shocked by it all that she didn't even bother to help herself. She just watched everything from the floor.

There was the mother, her hands gesturing, blurring, moving fast, fast, as she ranted in Sal's face.

There was Sal. Taking it.

Stacy looked for the girl. There was the father bending to her, his mouth moving, his hands sliding to the child's red cheeks. Stacy thinking it would be nice to crawl in Sal's lap like that, be comforted.

Someone out of sight yelled, "Don't move her."

Another voice, "We've called 911."

The child crawling into the father's arms, tangling herself there. Fine. "Madeline," he whispered into her blonde curls. Stacy somehow able to hear the name even as the mother screeched and screamed, an angry noise, the word "lawsuit" climbing in and out of her fat mouth like a rat.

Stacy blinked.

There was Sal trying to calm Dye-Job down, comping the meal and copying down their information, name, phone, address, and Stacy wondered if the mom would ever bend to the crying girl, would ever let Sal alone.

She heard the glass doors in the front banging open, and dark blue pant cuffs and black shoes moved into her line of sight.

Someone helped her up, checked on her, put her in a booth, left her there. Stacy put her head on the table and closed her eyes, only half listening to the rest of it. Everything hurt and the grease paint was starting to itch. She just wanted to sleep.

She shouldn't have taken that hit of acid from the bus boy.

She should have gone to college, like a normal person. Majored in art. Studied. Been something.

Later, she watched Sal's hands as he shoveled ice out of the Coke machine and packed it into a worn, white bar rag. They were long hands, with hard, angled knuckles and lovely dark skin the color of cherry wood. His palms were thick pads, the left cracked with yellow-white wrinkles, old burns. On the nights that the hard edges of those scars moved across her body, she'd shiver and hope they left a trail, some marking.

"How's it look?" Her voice rasped.

He quartered the rag's corners over the ice. "Bruising black. Must hurt like hell. You sure you don't want to go to the emergency room? I can't believe they didn't take you, too."

"I'm okay. Besides, don't want to." Everything came out as a half sound, alien. "No insurance."

He nodded. They both knew if he filed an official report to the Hut, if they reported her injury, the fight, she'd get fired.

They were alone. The restaurant had cleared soon after the ambulance left, and despite the fact that they were not yet closed, Sal had turned off the outside lights and sent everyone home.

For her.

She sat on the counter and tried not to wince as he put the ice against her throat. She imagined a bruise climbing across the pale of her skin. In her mind, she saw it, a grey-black stain sliding across his fingers, mixing pigment with pigment and painting her skin beautiful to match his.

She felt dizzy, thought of the girl. The poor kid.

The paramedics assured everyone that Madeline seemed fine, pupils the same, no bleeding, good reflexes, but just in case. The father had nodded, calm by then, his eyes on the window where he could watch his wife smoking outside. Finally, the ambulance had pulled away, Stacy heard the frightened child bawling from the back of it.

She wondered if she could call the hospital and find out if the girl was okay. Wondered if anyone would tell her anything. And she needed to tell them how she was just trying to help. It wasn't her fault.

She wanted to ask Sal about calling, but talking hurt.

He cupped the back of her head gently, and she hoped he'd kiss her, that his fingers would curl into her hair and he'd look into her eyes before leaning in. But he didn't, never really had, despite all of their time in the cooler. Not on the lips. Not sweetly. Not like that.

Then she realized she was still in the onesie.

She tried to say, "I must look sexy," a little joke, but stopped after "I must." Why bother? Finally she just said, "I think I should go home. I don't feel great." Her broken voice barely there.

"I got this," Sal said.

Stacy knew she shouldn't leave him to close the restaurant all by himself, to sweep and mop, to clean the make table, put up the salad bar, count the till, rinse the Coke nozzles. She started to protest, but he reminded her that he could always call his wife to come help close.

So there was that.

She asked Sal for a little water and when he turned to get it, she folded and palmed the scrap of paper he had written the couple's information on. She didn't even slip it into her purse. Instead, she held the tightly folded square, digging its dull corners into her palm.

He turned back around and stepped close, his body cradling into her, but instead of taking the water he offered, she pulled herself off the counter, her back scraping the edge as she slid down. She breathed out, and her small breasts touched his chest.

He laughed a little and tugged at the clown suit. "Sort of cute on you," he said, then, "You going to be okay?"

"Yeah. Sure."

The drive home was thankfully short. Even so, the old street was littered with road kill, the area having grown too big too fast. In five miles, she saw a possum, a cat, even a white whooping crane, twisted and broken, probably hit while fishing in the wet ditches by the road. People say they mate for life, but Stacy knew that was a myth, that there was no crane in mourning, no lifelong mate stalking the side of the road. She felt bad for it anyway.

And, God, she hurt.

Each pothole lent a throb to her throat, and when she pulled into her parking spot, she leaned her forehead against the steering wheel and tried to breathe. Feeling like the air was so much broken glass, she considered the pills in her pocket. Hydrocodone—parting gifts from the bus boy.

She took a swig from the beer Sal had poured into a to-go cup for her and fumbled for a pill.

The apartment was empty. Her four roommates were all at work, she guessed, or having fun. They'd been friends in high school. In theater and yearbook together, had gone to Mardi Gras and concerts. She'd had plenty of good, real friends then. Now, they never saw each other. Busy. Work. Life. Mostly they just paid rent together. The place smelled, a mix of gym clothes and weed, and Stacy gagged a little, making her throat hurt worse. She'd asked them not to smoke inside, but no one listened.

She found the couch, a thrift store reject, and waited for the Hydrocodone to kick in, the cold beer soothing her in the meantime. The paper, still curled in her hand, was damp. She didn't unfold it, just played with it, eyes closed, head tilted back on the couch, enjoying the way the booze and pills made everything fuzzy.

She'd watched enough television cop shows to decide that the little girl had probably been abused. That acting out was a sign. She heard half the kids out there were abused. Practically half. Something like that. She'd often wondered, watching those shows, if she herself had—something. Maybe she'd repressed the memories. Maybe that was why she was so fucked up. But, no. Her perfect parents had done nothing worse than be busy. And even then, she'd never been so much as neglected. But this little girl, butt in the air, panties on display, a kid like that was obviously in trouble.

She dozed.

When she woke up, she couldn't find the folded square of paper. It wasn't in her hand anymore, wasn't on the couch or the floor. Her heart pushed against her lungs, and there was no air.

She didn't know what she was going to do with the information on the paper, but she knew it was important. Madeline—No, Maddy— needed her. Maybe.

Maybe Maddy needed her.

The alliteration made her giggle, but the words tumbled across her thoughts, wouldn't let go. It seemed possible. Probable. She thought of the girl dancing, ass high in the air, her father's lips buried deep in her curls. Oprah had done a show on such children. Over-sexualized, bound to grow up wrong.

The paper!

She stumbled off the couch and looked between the cushions. Empty. She looked in the bedrooms. The roommates were still all gone.

She thought of calling Sal. Maybe the parents had called, left their information again when he said he couldn't find it. Would Sal understand though? Would he see that Maddy needed her?

Sal was at home with his wife by now.

She stumbled into the bathroom. Didn't bother with the mirror. Scrubbed at her face with a musty towel.

Her throat, her head, everything hurt.

She went into her room, called Sal, didn't hang up when the wife answered. "Sal," she said, still sounding broken, raspy.

The woman's voice stumbled with sleep. "Who is this?"

"I need Sal. I need to talk to him."

But when Sal finally got on the phone, he said, "Who is this," echoing his wife's words, the thick sleepy sound of her, and Stacy could think of no answer.

She pictured them in bed together. Him and her, him and his wife. She hung up.

In the kitchen, she found where one of the roommates had clipped her little folded paper to a note on the fridge, and clutching it once again, followed a double hydrocodone with a cherry popsicle chaser.

She finally fell asleep, fully asleep, not just passed out, and she dreamed of the girl. Nothing really happened in the dream, but Madeline was there, sweet face upturned so that the light caught it just so, dirty and sad. When she drifted awake, Stacy thought it was like the faces of the children in those advertisements for overseas charities.

Just a dollar a day.

For less than a cup of coffee.

You can make a difference.

Stacy knew she could indeed make a difference.

She considered calling the police. An anonymous tip. "Molesters," she'd say. "Beast of a couple," she'd whisper, "Real asshats."

But then she'd never see Maddy again. A bad idea. She knew that she had to see her again, just to know she was all right.

And—well, she was the only person who'd recognized the girl's plight. It gave them a special bond. Maddy would want to see her again. See the woman who saved her, maybe. Everyone loved a hero.

She pushed Sal's number into her phone.

He answered this time.

"It's me," her voice a little better today. "Stacy."

There was silence. Then, "Did you call last night?"

"No," she said. "I mean, yeah." Stacy looked down. She was still wearing the clown suit. She fingered a pink stain across the chest. Popsicle.

"Shit, girl. You're going to get my balls chopped off. You can't call that late."

Stacy found the last pill in her pocket, swallowed it dry before saying, "Can you meet me somewhere?" She felt the pill poking at the edges of her throat.

Sal was quiet.

"Please? Last night fucked me all up. I just want to talk to someone." She knew she was whining, but couldn't stop.

"It's just." He coughed a little.

Stacy listened to his silence and, over that, the rumble of highway sounds. He was taking her call outside, so no one could hear. Of course. She heard tires screeching nearby, imagined being hit by a car, that the screeching was someone desperately trying to stop, to not kill her. "Right. I shouldn't have—"

"No, you're fine." Sal always nice. "Of course you're shook up. Any other day. It's just today isn't...you know." More silence.

Stacy knew it was her turn to talk, said, "Right, right." She sucked in a breath, felt it burn like scotch as it traveled past her bruised pipes. "The girl?"

"No word. Must be fine." Stacy could imagine his smile here. Straight white teeth, full lips. "No worries, kid."

She tried to sound like she was also smiling. Pulled her lips backward. "I didn't mean to. It was an accident."

"Sweet thing like you? Of course it was." She imagined the smile again. Saw Sal turning it to the noisy highway outside his apartment, already moving out of the conversation. Sal was like that, always on the move. "Okay, kid."

She gnawed at her lip until there was a salty taste there, blood. "Okay," she said after he'd hung up.

Maddy's neighborhood was not far. Stacy found it on a map she picked up at the Circle K. She'd never read a map before. There was always someone to ask. Sitting in the convenience store parking lot, she was proud of this small accomplishment, reading a fucking map. She'd also purchased an Icee and, smiling at the cashier, a guy she knew from high school, some pocket pills.

He'd winced at the sight of her. "What the hell happened?" he said.

"A bitch throat-punched me at work."

He just looked at her, blinking. Handed her the drugs. "Diazepam," he said finally, "You know, Valium. They won't help with the pain. But they might relax you a bit. I don't have anything stronger." She left him the Icee.

In the parking lot, she took two of the round yellow pills and tried to fold the map shut. It wasn't far at all. She pulled her hair into a clip and realized how greasy it had gotten. Started the engine, rolled the windows down. She should have showered. She wondered now if the guy's wince had been for her angry bruise or something else, thought of the popsicle stains on her clown suit. Should have changed.

She took another pill, tried to think of the best route. The map showed a little park at the edge of Maddy's neighborhood. She headed that way. She thought of how much she'd loved swinging when she was a child. Loved flying so high that you could put your hand out against the clouds and pretend to touch the birds.

Such a nice day.

It was the sort of park that they built into a neighborhood, small and shady, with a set of swings and some monkey bars and a warped metal slide. Live oaks heavy with Spanish moss outlined everything. She had grown up with trees like that in her yard, a nicer neighborhood than this one. Here the trees were only at the park, but they were old and beautiful, too nice for where Stacy lived now. The family must be doing all right. She pulled past the parking lot and onto the service road that ran parallel, stopped there behind the oaks, unsure of what came next.

She cut the engine, played with the keys in her lap. Even with the windows cracked, the car was hot, made her drowsy.

She thought of how pretty Maddy was, imagined pushing the child in a swing, how people would smile at her, assume she was the little girl's mother.

The sun beat furiously at the windshield, the cotton clown suit, long sleeved, long pants, felt heavy. So hot.

She closed her eyes. Just for a bit. Then there was a noise, and she was awake, watching Maddy on the swings. A miracle.

She saw the child in spurts, the angle of the tree blocking the view so that it was like the little girl was flying through the oaks, head bandaged, fluttering skirt, that laugh, her body framed against the blue of the sky.

Stacy watched her flight and imagined she felt the whoosh of air as Maddy's feet arced towards her, felt a sucking as she swung back away.

She thought of Sal, his hand on her cheek, the biting cold of the ice as he fixed her. Thought of the whooping crane, all alone, its shattered wings at odd angles on the road.

Swallowed another pill. Another.

Felt Sal sliding away as she went to kiss him.

Took another.

Watched Maddy's skirt flutter through the leaves of the oaks, then pull away again and again.

It was so hot.

Stacy closed her eyes and rolled up the windows, wrapping the heat around herself, panting a little now, her breath moving in time with the swinging, up, down, in, out. She watched the child fly.

Took another pill, the child becoming blurry.

Alone in the car, Stacy imagined she could hear the heat, a whooshing, the blood pounding in her ears, the sound of Sal panting in the cooler, the noise echoing around in her like a bird's wings slamming against sliding glass doors, confused, trying to get in, trying to get out.

Elma

Elma set her cigarette on the edge of the soap dish. She examined her thinning hairline in the mirror, examined her ears, left eye, right, lifted each breast, ran her fingers across the skin her husband loved to nuzzle before his death. She put the cigarette back in her mouth and sat bare-assed on the commode to check her feet, between her toes.

There was a tick. Somewhere.

Or bedbugs. Lice. Bot flies. Fleas. Mites. Scabies.

She itched. Not just her skin. Her brain. The sharp, fiberglass splinters of last night's television, *Parasites: Monsters on Your Skin*, lodged there, pricking.

She knew it was the show driving her nuts. The new nurse had put it on. "Do you mind?"

She liked the girl. Never in a hurry. Elma'd learned to ask about their days. To offer tea. To keep new ailments to herself or they'd nurse-up the whole night.

On her inspection, she skipped the painful area behind her knee. The one she'd been ignoring. Keeping quiet about. That patch, sore to the touch for a month at least, wriggled and writhed, but she didn't look.

Instead, she scrubbed ticks from her hair. Mites from her breasts. Scabies off her skin. Even when she nicked the spot with her nail and the beetles tumbled out—again—their hard carapaces clicking against the tile floor, the last one catching, pinching on the way out of the wound, even then, she kept flicking her hair, fingering her scalp, searching, never looking down.

The Revival

They were in this sad little motel on the edge of Vidalia, and it stank of crack and weed and fried food, everything smothered in the smell. Maggie knelt like a girl praying, her stomach pressed up against the sharp edge of the tub, water sloshing everywhere. Bouie's fat fingers were rough against her skull. He pushed her head into the tub again and again, each time shifting his palm around. All the while, he kept clucking his tongue a little, just like he used to when they were kids swinging at imaginary baseballs in his auntie's yard. Finally, Maggie felt him settle on the base of her neck, meaty fingers tangling in her curls. Every time he allowed her head to clear the water, she arched her back, pushed out her chin, and flipped her dark hair, a mix of water and tears sliding prettily down her cheeks.

She wanted to get it just right.

They'd been dunking for about half an hour. She kept her eyes wide open, the water stinging like hell, and her sobs quiet, pulsing, coming out in small, raptured hiccups. She'd practiced crying like that in front of the mirror night after night. Knew how to make her breath short, shallow sounding. A little stutter. A little gasp. She thought maybe she'd smile at the end. Just the front teeth. Tried it. Then she shivered a little, shaking rivulets of cold water down the front of her dress.

Man, wearing that good little Baptist dress gave her a spark. Made her feel dirty. It was cut from milky white linen and had a boat-neck collar and no sleeves. Maggie liked the way it showed off the curve of her shoulders, the angle of her chin, barely hinting at everything else—when dry. But it was soft and thin and unlined, and that prissy Baptist dress went clear as glass once it was wet—her nipples showing sweet and pink right through the bath water. It was her wet breasts, free of bra or even gravity, that were Maggie and Bouie's secret weapon—the perfect bait for the poor, redneck sons of shrimpers, farmers, and single, grocery-packing mommas.

"Little lost lambs to the last," she'd say when they scouted a town, her eyes peeking over her sunglasses at packs of broad, out-of-work young men. Maggie always peeking over those glasses at things, day or night. Always practicing her Lolita, despite the fact that she was nearing thirty.

She liked to call them the lost boys, those aimless men. They were easy to spot, talking and drinking in deserted parking lots long after the bars closed, their Chevys and Fords waxed and glittering under the fluorescents, their girlfriends and mommas waiting in frayed easy chairs at home.

She spit out some water. The faint taste of sulfur sat on her tongue, and she spit again, snorting a little as she imagined herself waiting for one of those boys under a fucking crocheted blanket in some Goodwill easy chair. Bouie shifted his grip from her neck to her breast, and Maggie let it sit there for a minute, cupping her. It used to be, she'd swat at him when he got handsy, but only a week ago, when they were tooling around up in Natchitoches, she saw Bouie slip his knife between the ribs of a big, old corn-fed boy and then walk away without even a blink. He was getting meaner as they got older, she'd realized, cautious with him ever since.

"We got to focus," she said, digging her nails into her palm. "Come on." He gave her a little squeeze, and Maggie resisted the urge to jab him in the eye with her thumbnail. When they were kids she might have done it.

She counted and waited for Bouie to let go of her. He didn't, and she imagined slamming his head into the dirty tub. Imagined him dissolving in the gray water, how lonely that would be for her.

Finally, she yanked her tit from his paw. Bouie smiled a little.

"Where we going to dunk?" she said, grabbing a towel and struggling to her feet. Bouie didn't even put out a hand to steady her, and she wobbled some. Her knees hurt, were dimpled and red from all the kneeling. She rubbed them and curled her lip at him. "Well?"

He stepped out of the bathroom. "You'll tell them to meet us near that river we passed on the way in." His broad back all that was facing her anymore. "I went down there while you were in town. There's a narrow spot with a sandy bank that's easy to cross, near a mile from the road." Bouie flopped on the bed, turned on the TV. "We can start out with me on one side and you and the mouth-breathers on the other, then a 'halleluiah, halleluiah,' pass the plate, and you come on across, dunk, dunk. Then we pass the plate again. You doing it this time, catching the coin in your skirt, I guess."

Maggie nodded. "All wet."

"Next night, we give them an encore."

She pushed her hair into a makeshift bun. "I don't love the idea of wading through no backwoods bayou," she said. "Fucking snakes and gators and shit."

"Don't be such a pussy." Bouie always cool. The whole thing had been his idea—he'd heard his auntie lamenting the fact that the old tent revivals never came around anymore and figured the two of them could fill the void. Make a little bible scratch.

"Give big daddy a kiss," he said, grabbing his crotch.

She thought about his knife, the pearl handle slick with the corn-fed boy's blood and didn't tell him to fuck off. But Bouie'd been grabbing his dick and saying shit like that for years. The two of them just that way. They joked. "How about a beer?" Maggie made herself smile. There was a six pack of Schlitz icing down in the sink. She grabbed two and tossed him one, giving it a shake. That too—they'd been shaking cans at each other since they were maybe eleven. Everything they did, something they'd done before.

Bouie caught the beer, gave her the stink eye, and she took a pull from her own can. "Hot as it's been, the river will be warm as a bath."

"Good. Wouldn't want you to catch no cold." He flipped the channels until he hit ESPN. "Your whore momma'd tan me if I let you get sick."

"Shut up about my momma."

Maggie'd gone to live with Bouie and his auntie when she was in elementary, after her momma was caught getting high and "entertaining". The porch light of their little shotgun house had been rigged with a red bulb, and everyone, even Maggie, knew what it meant. Nights it was on, Maggie stayed out, the men her momma entertained not happy to be interrupted. So she played in the neighbor's deer corn until late, sometimes even camping out there. Bouie would maybe sneak out to join her, the two of them lying down in the warm ruts between the stalks, swinging their flashlight to see bucks' and does' eyes shining green as they crunched the corn.

Bouie always rubbing her back if she cried into the mud.

Maggie patted her nipples. Her momma used to spread lipstick on her own, never shy about Maggie watching her get ready. "With this heat, the girls might not perform." She took another drink of beer. "Maybe a dab of Prep H to make 'em pucker."

Bouie shrugged, "It's your tits." He turned the volume up on the game, and she knew that was the end of it. LSU was playing.

Maggie glanced at the clock and at Bouie, his eyes sleepy despite the announcers going nuts over some pass or something. She grabbed the rest of the six pack, leaving him only ice, and moved to the little walkway outside their room. She sat on the concrete, skirt pushed high on her thighs, and slid her legs through the slats of the railing, swinging her bare feet over the parking lot. Waiting.

It was the same every town. She'd find herself one of those lunch joints specializing in big servings, poboys or plate lunches or gumbo, the kind that advertised cheap Bud Light with your meal, and she'd sit near the front door a few days in a row. Maybe a week, sometimes two if the locals were slow to notice. At night she'd walk, all wide-eyed and trembling, into dive bars with pool tables, televisions, and pickled eggs. She'd sit with her ankles crossed, prim as could be, sipping water, her gin flask only coming out in the bathroom.

It was never long before a guy bit, his courage all screwed up into a knot pushing his chicken chest out. She'd smile with her mouth open just a little, showing the tip of her tongue, a bit of her teeth, and tell him all about angels, all the while looking like a mix of angel and sin herself. But those strutting boys were only 50/50 at best. Sure a lot would show up for the dunking, especially the ones out of work, curious and looking for something to believe, but their wallets might be tight.

The key was the shy boys. She'd watch for the ones who stared but didn't talk, who scooted their seats a millimeter closer each night.

When they were ripe and ready, hard-ons straining their work khakis whenever she bent over, she'd wait for them in the parking lot. Alone, trembling and peeking over her glasses, she'd maybe need a ride or, even better, protection from a stranger, claiming this guy or that had touched her "inappropriately," the word a drawn out whisper too close to a shy boy's reddening ears. And after a good week of her showing up in his diner, his bar, his dreams, that shy boy'd do damn near anything for Maggie.

Last night had only been a little different. A kid in a long jacket following her outside instead of finding her there. Putting his hand on her like he owned her. That black hole of a jacket, crazy in this heat, touching her thighs.

Just a little different.

She'd always say she was hungry, get them to talk all night over cooling coffee. These days, she'd tell them all about finding God. She'd sob a little, Maggie a good crier, and each and every time, she'd say that she'd never done this before, opened up like this. Whoever they were, they'd nod, they'd all nod, and Maggie figured every goddamned one of these lost boys must have waited his whole fucking life to grin and nod at her like that, like a goddamn bobble head.

That was how it was supposed to go, anyhow.

She counted eighty-four stars and named two new constellations before Bouie popped his head out of the room, looking for a beer. Eighty-four stars before she heard a gunning V8 below her.

Timing.

She hadn't planned on Bouie being out there when that motor revved its hello, Bouie's thick arm resting on the door all casual, the elastic on his boxers sliding below his belly. But she'd taken all the beer, hadn't she? So maybe she had planned on it. Her momma'd say, "Freudian slip-up." Maggie not sure if she wanted him to be jealous or it was something else, but sort of liking him catching her. Sort of hating it. A little scared of him these days.

"Hear that?" Bouie said. "That squeaking?"

"Yeah." Maggie was trying to look at Bouie and not over the railing, like the motor meant nothing to her.

"Mag-gie?" A voice like a cattle call cut between them.

Bouie didn't blink though. Kept his arm high on that door, leaning into it. "Your fella has a belt slipping down there."

The car gone quiet.

Bouie smiled a little, like he did for the mouth-breathers. "You heading somewhere? Got yourself another town boy with a bitchin car?" She didn't like it when he talked to her like that. Condescending. His broad, honest face making the tone even harder to take, like maybe you really were that stupid.

The other voice called, "Girl?"

Maggie pulled herself up. "A beat up Chevelle. Sad really, a car like that." Standing up had somehow put her a step closer to Bouie than she wanted to be, and she leaned back on her heels. A little bit more space. He seemed even bigger since he knifed that boy, not like when they were kids and they were the same. "It something to you?" she said, knowing that not telling him about asking the kid to come pick her up had made it weird, made it something to both of them. Their whole lives, she'd always told him everything.

She stopped her leaning and planted her feet. The beer made her hot. The thrill of him catching her draining out, replaced by something else. Feeling froggy, one of her momma's regulars called it. She pushed her chest forward, a schoolyard fighter puffing. "Jealous?"

Bouie smiled that preacher smile, "Don't you look all badass? Hell, I know whoring is in your blood. You just can't help yourself." He moved his arm off the door finally, standing straight, and she liked that. It made him seem less like a cat pretending to bathe before a fight. "You just remember what we're here for." He paused. "And you keep that whore mouth shut, kid." Reminding her he was older, in charge.

"Yeah," she said, grabbing the last couple of beers and turning away, leaving him none.

Footsteps on the stairs. "Girl?"

"Stop fucking calling me that," Maggie said. "I'm coming." She waved the beers at Bouie like some sort of good-bye and kept a watch on his shadow to make sure he didn't follow her down the stairs. Bouie stayed put.

All the way down, though, she watched the ground for a shift in the darkness and thought about how she'd already opened her damn whore mouth.

Fingering Bouie's knife in her pocket the whole damn walk.

The thing about the corn-fed boy up in Natchitoches was that he'd been crushing on her, following her around, trying to slip his hand into hers once in a while.

And once in a while, she'd let him.

He hadn't been a mark, though. He was just a guy they got to help hand out fliers, haul chairs, pass the plate, yell halleluiah. Just a plant in the congregation, a friend of Bouie's cousin. A guy who was good for keeping his mouth shut and being strong. Dumb and sweet like a good dog, and Maggie had thought she might keep him around.

So she told Bouie, and he'd nodded, and not much later the kid was holding the hilt of that knife in his belly, blood slipping over his hands, brighter than Maggie imagined blood could be, brighter than a busted nose or lip or the gush from your tongue after a good smack bangs it against your teeth. So bright it made her eyes sting.

Then Bouie pulled his knife out of that corn-fed boy and handed it to her to clean off, the pearl handle so slick that she almost dropped it.

The kid's blood smeared her hands, stained her shirt. When Maggie hid her face so Bouie wouldn't see her crying, blood painted her forehead and cheeks. A little even got in one eye.

And then they'd just left Natchitoches, the boy still bleeding on the street for all Maggie knew.

But this new guy was different. Not like the sweet corn-fed kid at all. Maggie'd been around bad men all her life and she knew how they moved, easy, easy. That's why she'd grabbed Bouie's knife. Just in case. True, this one was barely more than a baby, no man at all, but he moved smooth as hell. Sleepy looking, really. Even driving, his fingers were light on the wheel, the shifter, like he needed to make sure he could move his hands fast, just in case.

When he'd stopped her in the bar parking lot the night before, she'd seen hatred, rage in him. Wondered if he'd meant to rape her. He looked the sort of special crazy that might would do more. He put his hand on her arm, gripping her so she felt his nails, and smiled a little, his lips wrapped tight across his teeth. He smelled too sweet, like his sweat had gone bad, rancid. "You're new here," he said.

But instead of pulling away, Maggie had leaned into him. "Yup, and aren't you strong?"

The kid caught off guard by that.

"Thought I'd squirm?" she asked him, her mouth too close to his ear. "Struggle?" Her sunglasses pushed hard into his cheek. "Thought you scared me?" She crushed her chest into him, her tongue into his ear, her nails into the flesh above his crotch.

He looked about sixteen and Maggie guessed he'd never, ever imagined a girl like her.

"Drop my arm and maybe you'll get something nice out of the deal."

And he did. Maggie the biggest predator in the lot.

When she saw that she had him she took the kid out, told him all about the revival, maybe too much about it. The kid's eyes got all glossy, his breathing quick. Then sometime, later that night, she told him to pick her up at her hotel the next evening, liking this new dangerous toy.

Now here they were, pulling into the Eighty Four Kwik Thru. Maggie told him she was starving when he picked her up from the motel and even this frothing dog obeyed, found her food.

"Not a lot open at night," he said, climbing out of the Chevelle.

They ate Fritos in the field behind the convenience store, and she watched the folds of her skirt curl around his hand as he moved it up her leg.

She thought about Bouie bossing her, and wanted him to understand how powerful she was, wanted him to see the way she owned this kid. She wanted Bouie to be just a little afraid, like she was. To feel like she felt ever since he took the corn-fed boy away from her.

So she parted her thighs a little and told the kid how he felt strong, like God Almighty. She bit his shoulder so hard he bled and told him about how Bouie pawed at her, how she sort of belonged to the big guy. She whispered into his ear that it was like Bouie took her from Jesus and made her his own.

And then, how much he, this rabid mutt kid, glowed with the Lord.

The night before she'd noticed how lit the kid got when she said they were doing revivals, how he'd sweated as he'd muttered, "out of the mouth of the dragon."

So she'd said between bites, "You're like the fury of God himself. Like you could pull me back to the light." Then she said, "This has to be the only time," as she eased him out of his jeans. She bit the kid there too. Made sure he didn't finish. That he'd come back for her.

Bouie was awake when she returned, the kid in the jacket sent home, a little happy, a little frustrated.

"Have fun?" Bouie asked, pointing that preacher smirk at her.

Maggie went and sat on the edge of his bed, then lay down next to him, her over the cover, him under. She put her head on his chest. "You remember when Bobby Ray called me a whore in the tenth grade?" Maggie listening for the way his heart had this extra little thump every few beats.

Bouie put his hand on her forehead, not stroking her, just laying it there, like she knew he would. Everything they did, something they'd done a million times before. "I'm sorry I called you and your momma whores," he said. He didn't sound terribly sorry.

"You held him down so I could break his nose." Maggie closed her eyes. Smiled. "Then you bandaged my hand, got all the Bobby Ray snot out of my busted up knuckle."

"Yup."

"Thank you for that."

Bouie's chest moved under her as he shrugged, and they fell asleep like that, as chaste as children. Then somebody had her by the hair, was flinging her off the bed. Her head hit the wall. She tried to figure out the black blur, the panting.

It was the kid in the jacket. "Mine," he screamed.

Now she was on the floor, and the kid was on Bouie, straddling the big man and wailing into him. His arms were those skinny, wiry things that could explode into violence, and Bouie's face was soon swollen and bleeding. Maggie wondered how the fight would have gone had Bouie not been asleep.

The kid screeched over and over, "Wake up, you cocksucker!"

Bouie, obviously awake now but dazed, struggled to get his hand between the mattress and the box springs, fingers wiggling, searching. Finding nothing, Bouie expanded his chest, pushed himself upward in a burst, but the kid held on, a real cowboy in his black duster.

Maggie rubbed her head where it had hit the wall. Found blood there. Smiled a little.

Bouie finally freed himself enough to throw a punch. A real winner. The kid rocked backward with the force of it, and Maggie wondered if it made him hard, that type so turned on by the fight. And she wasn't surprised to see the kid's hand disappear for a moment into his duster, but Bouie sure looked surprised to see his own knife coming out of there.

Then the kid was wailing again, this time with the knife, blow after blow ripping down into Bouie. The fierceness of it more than anything

Maggie could of imagined. And she tried not to see the pale blue of her partner's fingernails as his arms thrashed about, rarely blocking a blow. Suddenly realizing how fragile he might be.

Now Maggie was up and running from the violence. Into the bathroom. Hand behind the toilet. Her mother's derringer there. Locking the door only after it is in her hand. Fumbling out her cell phone with the other. Falling backward into the tub, crouching in there. Gun shaking. Thumb hitting 911.

Maggie such a good crier.

When the sirens came, she whispered over and over to the operator, "I'm so scared. I'm so scared," as the police screamed "surrender," into their bullhorn.

The room shook with the sound of repeated fire. The kid never giving up—something she should have realized about him. But maybe she had, way back in her mind.

She wondered what she'd do without Bouie.

As she waited, she pushed her fingers into the soft pain in the back of her skull and blessed how head wounds bled. No one could see all that red and think she did this. The police found her in the bathtub, the blood from where she'd hit her head on the wall smudged in a streak across the sweet Baptist dress. She made herself small in the tub, looking young and afraid, until one of the men coaxed her with a cool wet rag, bathing the blood from her face and head, the water dripping pink into her lap.

"Paramedics are coming," the cop said.

"God bless you." Maggie wrapped her fingers around his hands, pushing them close to her face so that the washcloth, now stained, all but obscured her upturned eyes.

Naturallique

Tyler had been drunk, fully drunk, for ten and a half days when Sweetie Clark knocked on his door. There she was, standing on his porch—just standing there as if it were the most normal thing you could imagine—looking bored and sweaty and searingly beautiful, barely two weeks after Genevieve told him that she was leaving. Their twenty-year marriage, "O-V-E-R."

Sweetie Fucking Clark, standing there like a gift from god.

When he was thirteen, Tyler reached for his French horn just as Sweetie went for her clarinet, the two of them rocking on their tiptoes in the band closet. As she jostled the instruments on the top shelf, his forearm, still sticky from Phys Ed, slipped under her early double D's, every bit of her touching him. He could even feel the ribbing on her tank top. It was Tyler's first brush with breasts. For months, the surprising weight of Sweetie burned at him, haunting his flesh.

She'd sashayed in and out of his dreams for years after, even making an unexpected appearance on his wedding night as he lounged, alone, in the hot tub, Genevieve having wrapped herself in a hundred-dollar nightie and a handful of sleeping pills. And now, the real, live Sweetie Fucking Clark was standing next to Gene's old world roses, Tyler imagining their smell as hers.

For the first time since Genevieve left, he stopped thinking of his wife folding her underwear, zipping her bag, patting his cheek a little too hard as she talked of taxis and lawyers and hotel rooms. Even the tequila had not given him that sort of relief.

"Package," Sweetie said. She was holding out not a package, which was under her arm, but an electronic pad for him to sign. She looked phenomenal in the UPS get-up. The brown shorts and top were a bit too tight on her thickened frame, so the stitching pulled, acting like arrows guiding his eyes. And he was thirteen again, sweating at the sight of her.

Sweetie shook the tablet at him a little, and Tyler became acutely aware that he was wearing Genevieve's robe. The silk flaps were wide open, his too-white belly, a sick moon thing, hanging over a pair of not-white-enough boxer briefs. "Sweetie?" he said, hoping it was very early morning so that the robe, the underwear, would seem less sad.

"Excuse me?"

"Sweetie Clark?" Tyler smiled, trying to get the flaps of the robe closed, "It's me, you know, um," the silence pulled between them. For chrissake, he couldn't remember his name. Finally, he just said, "me."

She squinted a little.

"High school." More silence. "French horn." Tyler tried to grab for the tablet, praying his name was there. The motion was more of a snatch than he'd meant, and Sweetie shifted back on her heals, got all squinty and very purposefully out of his reach.

"Ninth grade." Tyler made a noise, a sort of cat scratching at the back of his throat noise. "And tenth." He could feel himself blinking too fast. "Eleventh, too," he said.

"Yeah, okay." She shrugged and moved the tablet back towards him, "No one calls me Sweetie anymore." There was a little smile, a hint of adult braces under wide lips, "So, anyway, sign here, okay?"

Tyler looked over the pad. There was an X and a line on the screen. There were buttons, a cord, a pen, a series of nicks in the black plastic surface, but his name, his freaking NAME, was not there. His lips tightened, and he felt his chin beginning to shake a little. He begged himself not to cry. Not to be that band geek again. Then he remembered. "Comeaux," he said, too loud in that way he had, making her jump a little. "Tyler Comeaux."

She clearly did not remember him. "Okay."

Her polite, stiff-braces smile didn't change.

He signed the pad, took the package, closed the door. His stomach tightened, the high he'd felt on seeing Sweetie replaced by nausea. He dumped the box on the kitchen counter, knocking beer bottles onto microwave burrito sleeves, and headed for Genevieve's computer. Gene'd left everything behind except those few outfits she'd folded neatly into her luggage, even leaving a couple of bras damp on the shower rod. The first few days, Tyler thought that meant she was coming back, as if maybe she'd only left until her lacies were dry.

The screen told him it was 3:47 pm. "Call work—tell them not dead," said a yellow post-it he'd left on the keyboard. "Stop crying"—that was the one on the monitor. "Get dressed," was written on the crumpled note by the space bar. Gene had hated his post-its, found his short correspondences demeaning. "I'm not your fucking secretary," she'd said.

Tyler opened a browser, Sweetie Clark's tight UPS uniform nudging him on. He needed something, anything delivered. He found a mini kegerator (Genevieve thought they were stupid) and paid fifty dollars extra to have the beer fridge shipped express delivery. He hoped it would not be too heavy for Sweetie to carry, hoped they'd ship it soon.

It was the first thing he'd ever ordered online. Tyler didn't like computers much. He was tied to one at work, plugging in Medicaid resubmission codes and place of service codes and procedure modifier codes, and even the asshole-on-the-line codes that Smith, in the cubicle next to him, had made up. He didn't want to type type type on one at home, too.

It drove Genevieve crazy. She called him a self-hating Luddite because of how he avoided them, how he didn't have an iPhone, couldn't barely work the cable box. The package on the counter must be hers. She loved computers, loved to shop online. He grabbed the neck of the Cuervo and took a swig, wandered back into the kitchen, now curious.

His name was on the label, though, not Gene's.

It was a plain box, no logo, no company name, and the return address gave nothing away. He nudged it with his bottle and thought about how the cardboard had mashed down on Sweetie's breast, the corner making a bit of a dimple there, just below her nipple. Tyler ran the bottle along that corner, decided to open the box. Like a Russian nesting doll, it contained another box made of slick cardboard with thick walls, expensive looking and laminated pink. It even had dainty purple curls etched into the sides. In bold cursive, it said *Naturallique.*

Inside that box, coyly nestled in pink velvet, were six clear, round sacks. They quivered, filled with liquid or maybe gel. Breast implants, he was pretty sure. Code 19340 for implantation after mastectomy. He didn't think there was a code for having them delivered to your house. There were three pairs, three sizes.

A note card, embossed in pink and purple, encouraged him to consult his doctor once he'd chosen his perfect look. It also congratulated him on taking his first step to a happier, prettier him. No, no code for that. It wasn't a covered procedure. Finally, in smaller print, the letter gently reminded him that the enclosed implants were for consultation purposes only and, as they were unsterilized, were unsuitable for implantation (which, of course, should only be performed by a licensed physician). The logo at the bottom was a chesty silhouette.

Tyler was mesmerized. To be honest, he hadn't seen breasts in a long time. Coded them yes. Seen them, no. In the last years of their marriage, Genevieve only let him touch her through a layer of nightgown once or twice a month, until, eventually, he gave up on that as well.

"I'm a neuter, he's a neuter, wouldn't you like to be a neuter, too," he'd once sung to a window full of puppies while wandering through a strip mall on his lunch break. It was just the way things went, he guessed. Probably perfectly normal.

He took another pull at the tequila, grabbed the outer box, and checked the label again.

> Tyler Alexander Comeaux
> 1400 Walter Drive
> Lafayette, LA 70503

"Yup," he said, looking back at the glistening orbs. He went to poke one, one of the big ones. Moved in slow motion, finger hovering—as if he might get in trouble if caught. Finally, still feeling weird about it, he sunk his finger in. The artificial breast was like firm jello packed into a thick zip-lock bag. He pushed until his fingertip disappeared and the breast looked as if it might pop, bulging obscenely.

It was strangely, delightfully cold.

For the first time since Genevieve left, he picked up the phone, dialed work. He had few friends outside of the office and could think of no other number to try.

"Tyler!" Smith answered on the first ring. They mostly only talked over the cubicle wall, but he was a good guy. "How's France, buddy? We were worried, thought you'd be back by now." Tyler'd surprised Gene with a second honeymoon for their anniversary, handing her the card as she packed, the plane tickets and itinerary tucked inside.

He said to her, "See, see, we could go here," and then later that day, when he knew she was really leaving, "No, you take it. I bought it for you." Now, he wondered if she'd gone to France without him, imagined her eating bon-bons with a dashing, dark haired Frenchman at the Louvre.

"Tyler?"

"Did you mail me breasts?" he said into the handset, shaking Genevieve out of his thoughts.

"What?"

"Breasts. I have a box of breasts here."

"Tyler?"

"So, no?"

"Did you say breasts?"

"No...no. Never mind. I'm pretty drunk." Tyler poked at one of the smaller ones. It was also delightfully cold. The edges of Genevieve's hips had been like that, strangely, wonderfully cold, even during the worst of the summer heat. "France, you know. They keep you drunk here."

"Are you okay, buddy?"

Tyler considered saying, "No, Genevieve left me, and I have this strange box of breasts," but he couldn't bear to hear himself admit she'd gone. Instead he said, "Oop, cancan girl. Gotta go. Be home soon," pressed end, and threw the phone into the sink.

On their twentieth wedding anniversary, when Genevieve told him to sit on the bench at the end of the bed, he thought it was for something kinky. A present. Some of that Penthouse end-of-the-bed-bench sex. He went to unbutton his fly. She pulled a suitcase out and explained that their marriage was over. Tyler shifted around, not quite listening, hand paused on the top button. They'd had that bench for five years, and it was the first time he remembered anyone sitting on it. He was amazed at how torturously uncomfortable the damn thing was. Not good for sex. But that was what their marriage had become, precious mahogany benches that asses never touched. Certainly, not naked asses, and never, ever writhing, naked asses. What had he been thinking? Theirs was a life filled with sterile things. Towels too good for damp hands, genitals perpetually wrapped in high-quality underwear. Even pillows that had to be carefully placed in a chest before sleep, less either one of them shed a skin cell on their silk cases.

The bed was full of those freaking pillows.

Everything decorative, everything unused.

They'd met in college when she got trapped tutoring him in math. She was the sort of pretty he called stuck-up pretty back then, blonde hair that looked like it might be warm to touch, small, hard breasts tucked into prim shirts she'd actually starched and pressed.

She was so very out of his league that his palms didn't bother to sweat around her. So hot, she didn't seem to register as human. Or he figured he didn't. They weren't even the same species. But the first time that Tyler managed to factor a quadratic equation, she leaned over and kissed him. Giggling and saying, "You didn't even try to count to X on your fingers and toes," and then just pushing her lips against his as if they did that sort of thing. He'd acted like she'd called him Einstein, the thought of a girl like that liking him made nothing else matter.

But once the cloudiness of meeting, of sex, of generally being in love had worn off, once they were married and it was too late, he found out that they really didn't like each other. Still, after so long, he'd been surprised when she ended it.

To meet the taxi, to do the final bit of leaving, Genevieve put on her red heels, the ones Tyler had paid for in Paris the first time they went. The shoes clicked ridiculously against the cobblestone drive. He tried to figure out how many claims made for a pair of clicking Jimmy Choos. How many times he had to say, "I'm sorry, miss. You'll have to write a letter." How many shittastic red-eye flights to insurance conventions, exactly how much soul-crushing ass kissing was wrapped up in those fucking heels. But when she stumbled, he had to resist the urge to break free of the doorway and grab her bag for her, to steady her as her heel caught in the ruts.

She gave him the finger and Tyler tried not to cry.

He slipped inside and pushed his face deep into the 100 percent bamboo sheets that she so loved, just to smell her powder, the coconut from her shampoo, the thick cream she wrapped her hands in every night, and he wondered how often she washed the linens, wondered how he'd know when it was time to do it. He lay there alone, wondering why he'd never realized how warm she was at night, how the coolness of her right hip was a lovely surprise when she shifted her weight, how good she'd felt there at his back.

He slept on the couch after that.

It took a few days for the kegerator to come in, and by the time it shipped, Tyler had forgotten ordering it. Mostly he slept, but when he didn't, he stared at the breasts. He wondered if Genevieve had ordered them after all. If the name thing was just a mistake. He wondered what that would mean, her wanting silicone curves. Then, he thought maybe she sent the breasts to fuck with him, some sort of messed up joke he was too drunk to get.

He became obsessed. Thinking about them, trying to figure them out, touching them all the time. He was juggling the breasts when he got the idea. Large, medium, small, large medium, small, all six of them, the most balls he'd ever gotten in the air at once. He was feeling oddly smug about this feat when, in the smack, smack, smack haze of a perfect artificial breast juggle, he wondered what they'd feel like, *really feel like*, on. Which was how it happened that when he opened the door the morning the kegerator came in, he greeted Sweetie Fucking Clark wearing his wrinkled, dirty jeans and one of Genevieve's lace bras from the bathroom. He'd stuffed the bra to the brim with fake breasts, put all six of them in there, piled and lumpy, sticking out in strange, rolling bumps.

Somehow, it was the sloppiness of his man-breasts above his flabby stomach, one glistening sack stacked on another on another, that seemed like the worst part.

The corner of Sweetie's mouth rumbaed up and down, her lips tight over her braces. He knew that any moment that laugh would break free. She coughed a little, "Tyler Comeaux, right?"

Tyler nodded, squinting painfully as the summer sun poured around her dark curves, an eclipse of chest and elbows and hips. He moved his arm across himself in a small attempt to cover the bulging red lace.

She cleared her throat, lips still doing that dance. "French horn, third chair?" she said, voice crackling over the words.

He nodded again.

"Well, you look," she actually laughed out loud then—a hearty bark of a laugh—and Tyler remembered how he'd followed that sound around corners at their high school. "Sorry. I'm sorry. You look busy, is all." She pushed the electronic pad at him, still giggling a little.

He fumbled to sign and dropped the pen, thought it might be time to throw the tequila away. Maybe after he had enough to forget Sweetie laughing at him.

"Anyway," she waved at the box at her feet, "Something bigger for you today."

"Okay." He tried to hold her tablet in such a way that maybe, just maybe, it covered some of the bra.

Sweetie nodded. And nodded. And nodded. "Okay," she said. Then she just stood there, looking at him.

Leave, Tyler thought. *For god's sake, leave.*

They nodded at each other, Tyler trying to match his head bob to hers.

"Right," she said.

He adjusted his arm to get maximum coverage and shifted his gaze to the roses. The closest bush was dropping leaves. He felt his face getting hot as he remembered pouring the plant a shot of Cuervo sometime earlier that week. It took a lot of effort to keep his eyes pointed at the drooping plant and not at Sweetie, and then he felt a tug at his hand.

"I'm going to need that back, dude."

He was still holding the tablet. "Crap."

Tyler let go, and as Sweetie nodded one last time, laughter snapped back out of her.

"I'm really not a freak," he said, and for some reason, she smiled. Not the polite, tight smile, but a full-on look at the braces smile.

"Ok," she said, "See you, French horn, third chair." Halfway to the truck, she turned back around, "I think you probably only need one of those per cup," she yelled up the drive.

"Right," he called back, adjusting the strap on the bra. Then he heard his own voice, barely a squeak, trying out the words "my wife left me" on the tailpipe of the receding van.

That night, Tyler ordered a HoneyBaked Ham, a Fender guitar, an azalea (to replace the dying rose bush, the new plant just like the ones that grew like weeds around his childhood home), and a genuine replica of a T-Rex tooth. He was still wearing Gene's bra.

He'd decided that he had to show Sweetie he was not crazy, that he owned clothes, that he was maybe the sort of guy you could have coffee with—without the fear of being stabbed or asked to join a cult or something. He had to get her back to the house.

While he shopped, he removed one implant and then another, barely noticing the breasts piling around him. Sweetie slipped from his mind. He was amazed what you could get online. Sure, he'd known about the porn and the Nigerian princes with money to launder, but somehow he hadn't really realized everything else that was out there. Even when he used the internet, Tyler'd kept his sphere tight, sticking to work stuff and maybe watching a YouTube video of a singing cat at Smith's insistence every now and again.

Besides, Genevieve had been in charge of the shopping, replacing his shoes and pants with clockwork efficiency, buying his family's gifts at Christmas, and even picking him out a shotgun for the failed hunting trip with her dad.

And he'd let her.

He wasn't sure which one of them had started it, but life had gotten simple over the years. So simple to just look up and have new shoes, even if he hated brown suede, even if the toes pinched, even if they looked a little girlish. It was just easier. And Genevieve always took care of it. No problem.

But now, now, he clicked his way to Bed, Bath, and Beyond, buying thick looking guest towels that he'd use every single day, even if he was extra, work-in-the-yard sweaty. He clicked over to Brookstone where he bought a fat leather recliner with a cup holder built right in. He bought comic books and a video game system. He even found a place you could order pet fish, and soon he was filling a digital dream aquarium with exotics to be shipped from around the world.

He shopped until his credit card was declined.

"This is an odd way to stalk someone," Sweetie said when he opened the door. There were three boxes piled at her feet.

Tyler stepped outside and picked up the top box, shook it. "It's like Christmas," he said. He'd showered and was wearing his nicest khakis.

He'd even been sleeping in them so that there was no way Sweetie would knock while they were not on. Unfortunately, the only clean shirt he'd found was from a Ratt concert he'd gone to in 1990. It was a little short.

She laughed. "All right, then. Sign please?"

"I just wanted to tell you," Tyler did his best to smile in a non-threatening manner, "those weren't mine."

"The packages?"

Tyler blinked. "No." Suddenly, he was blinking too much, too fast. "No, no, no. The, you know," he waved a hand in a figure eight in front of his nipples, realized his voice was coming out excessively loud again. "They just sort of came in the mail, with you." He shifted around. The rose had dropped more leaves. "I mean, you didn't come in the mail, of course. You brought them. The breasts." He tried to look past her, tried to think about the grass that desperately needed mowing. He tried to shut up. Instead, Tyler mumbled, "You brought me the breasts."

Sweetie's lips began their little rumba, and she pushed her bangs out of her eyes. They were damp with sweat, and Tyler wondered how many houses she visited each day, how many before and after his.

"But, they weren't mine," he said.

She laughed, and he imagined he could feel the crackle of her full-throated laugh reverberating against his chest. He remembered how the other kids would tease her about that laugh, and how she'd just laugh right along with them, never holding any of it back. "You're an odd duck." She handed him the electronic pad. "But, you look like you're feeling better. Less vomit-y."

Standing next to her on the porch, Tyler could smell the soft scent of talcum powder. He shook his head, confused. "I wasn't—"

"Tequila does that to me, too, makes me green."

Tyler nodded. This was going differently than he'd planned. He signed the pad, handed it back, and Sweetie gave him the full braces smile. "You smell better, too."

Tyler noticed little lines digging into the skin around her eyes, the same lines that Genevieve scared away with Botox, and he noticed that the part in Sweetie's black hair was surrounded by scattered gray. Her skin, the soft shade of brown the other kids called "bright" back in high school, was marred in places by spots, bigger than freckles, dotting her cheeks.

Tyler tugged at the hem of his T-shirt, suddenly afraid that if he didn't occupy his hands, his fingers would leap to that face, brush her cheekbones, the tip of her nose.

He called Genevieve. He fished the phone from the sink and found it still worked and he called her cell, hoping she wasn't still in France. When she answered, he didn't say anything. Neither did she.

Tyler was pretty sure she knew it was him, so he stayed there on the line, just listening to the both of them saying nothing. She didn't hang up, but she didn't talk either.

He thought he could hear her breathing a little. Maybe it was just the echo of his own exhales playing back at him.

And then he started to cry. Little, unmanly noises, slipping out of him and into the phone and onto Genevieve, wherever she was.

And then there was a click.

He pulled off the khakis and climbed into the bed, pushing his nose into the sheets, trying to smell her there again. He pressed against all of her pillows and slept until the next day, when the knocking started all over.

Now, he regretted the packages.

He answered the door in the Ratt shirt, his underwear.

"My wife left me," he said, hearing failure in the words. "My wife left me and you're the only person I've told."

Sweetie looked at him, her mouth open just a fraction, and he couldn't tell if she was about to say something or was just breathing in the muggy air. She reached out and touched his shoulder, pressed her fingers firmly into him so he could just feel the tips of her nails through his shirt. They stood there like that for a moment.

"Sarah," he said, "I guess you're Sarah these days. Sarah Clark?"

She nodded, left her hand there, the pressure of it wonderful, grounding.

"I'll see you, Tyler Comeaux, third chair," she said, finally moving her hand with a small pat. She turned to leave, but smiled at him first, deepening the wrinkles at the edges of her brown eyes and flashing her braces at him. Tyler barely saw it. He was looking instead at a ragged bloom on the rose bush, the flower's edges dark and tattered from the summer heat.

He closed the door, wondering if he'd ever stop feeling tired. He gathered the breasts and went to the bedroom. The pillows first. Then, the sheets. Everything stripped. He was careful not to smell anything, not to hold anything too close. Not quite sure where Genevieve kept the extras, he lay down on the bare mattress. Then, propped on his elbow, Tyler arranged the breasts on Gene's side of the bed. He placed them in a sort of curving line near the middle, with one or two verging onto his side of the mattress, and then he slept there, uncovered, with his back to the silicone silhouette he made, every now and then bumping against one of the breasts as he shifted in his sleep.

Snake Oil

Manny'd changed the background on their computer again, and now deep blue waves curled around an island in the center of Lolo's screen. It looked like a jade carving set in spilled paint, the colors so saturated. She could feel his ache there, knew he saw a cruise or retirement or paradise in the picture he'd chosen. Lolo saw sharks and drownings and dengue fever. She saw death. She always saw death.

She opened a spreadsheet, maximizing the window so columns of numbers overtook her screen. Order. She didn't ever tell Manny that she didn't like the backgrounds, never changed them to something more comforting. "Do you think Henry and that girl, the redhead? You think they got something going?" she said. He was on the bed behind her, reading a spy novel. Escaping.

"Maybe."

Lolo wanted to point out the threat the girl could pose. The danger. But it was sometimes hard to gauge her responses to things—was she being melodramatic? Paranoid? So she said, "She's married, I think."

"Maybe."

Manny didn't believe his brother Henry's business was any of their business. "He lets us live here, baby," he'd say to Lolo whenever she bitched about Henry. "Give the guy some space," he'd say.

They paid rent, though. Not a lot when they moved in, it's true, but more every month as she made more. As the business she'd built for the three of them—that she'd damn well invented—took off. And Henry brought all his trouble to the house with him. Ridiculous parties she had to hide from. Married girls and their pissed off husbands. His loud friends so eager to show off their strength they wrestled right through the furniture, breaking anything not hidden away.

She didn't turn to face her husband. "You don't think that this is a bad idea?" she said. "I mean we can't have her just hanging out around here, seeing everything."

For once, Manny didn't shut her down. "I'll talk to him."

The bit of fenced yard behind Henry's wood frame house, so cloaked and shaded by twin oaks and pines that it almost felt like being inside, was one of the only outside spaces Lolo could still handle. She pulled a pack of Marlboro Reds from behind the Blessed Virgin's halo. She had to squat in the overgrown grass to ferret her lighter out of the nook where Mary's wimple met her gown, below her ear and behind the crest of her shoulder, the molded concrete cool and rough in the hollow there. She kissed the Virgin square on the head and pushed out of her squat, bending as if the arch of the sky loomed too low. "Momma, excuse my French," she said to the Mary, "but these needy cunts are going to be the death of me." She lit her cigarette and said a prayer, her eye on the house.

There were three women in there. The redhead and two others. They were the sort that, in high school, Lolo would have called the pretty girls. Hair perfectly messy in sporty topknots, jeans that looked tailored to dip and slouch around their curves, and white skin, tanned to a crisp, dark-but-not-too-dark gold. She didn't even know Red's name. The others were—no, she didn't know any of their names. In her head, they were all Jane: Fat Jane, Red Jane, and Smells like Onions Jane. The kitchen was so crowded the air became heavy, warm and damp and smothering, everyone's breath on her. Three women, her husband, his good for nothing brother, her little mutt Port (barking and coughing and carrying on in what sounded more like death throes than aggression), and five little Igloo coolers of donated breast milk.

Smells like Onions was a champion pumper. Two of those coolers were hers.

"Lolo? Did you find some?"

Lolo put the cigarette out on the bottom of her shoe and tossed it in the lilies edging her neighbor's ditch. What her husband Manny meant was, "Lolo, stop screwing around and get in here." He knew better than to say it, the way he knew better than to ask if she'd been smoking again, but after fifteen years, he didn't need to.

In her pocket was the "some" of what she'd offered to go forage for the women, their squawking sending her looking for an excuse to visit the Virgin and her Marlboros. She'd picked nothing more exciting than a handful of dandelion leaves that she passed off as blessed thistle—for milk production. God, they loved magic herbs. She neither had the thistle nor fully trusted its safety as far as their babies were concerned, and she drew a line there. Whenever they came, she picked the dandelions from the closest edge of the ditch, wild and unruly thanks to a dispute with the landlord, and told the Janes to add just a few leaves to a salad, "Really just a tiny few each meal."

At least they'd eat some vegetables.

Inside, Lolo affected an accent. Above her own faint southern roll, she folded a Hispanic lilt somewhere in between her Tia Espie's and one she remembered from a psychic commercial that played constantly when she was a child in Miami. Not a strong accent, just something a little more exotic than small town Louisiana generally got. "I found some," she said. "Not a lot. You will have to share." She draped the leaves across the counter as solemnly as she could. When she was little, her grandmother had draped rosaries she brought in from trips to South America and Europe in just the same way, the gesture gentle, her back bent as if in a bow. "My mama, god rest her—"

Manny coughed. It sounded a lot like he said "Jesus." Lolo didn't bother to shoot him a look. He knew better.

"She believed it was best to pick everything under a full moon." Lolo made a show of looking heavenward as if she could see either the moon or her mother (who was currently draped across a lounge chair on a half-priced cruise to Jamaica) through the popcorn ceiling in the rental. Then she laughed, a chicken noise so loud it startled poor Port, who took to wheezing. "But I don't think the plants are that picky. All right, ladies. You know the drill. Put it in your salad only."

Port jumped on Henry's lap and coughed out a look-at-me bark. Henry was making eyes at Red Jane instead of putting the breast milk in the fridge, and Lolo liked to believe Port was telling him to get off his ass, doing his duty as her loyal dog. In truth, he liked Henry, who roughhoused with him and took him on rides in the truck, better than he liked her. Everyone did.

Lolo checked Red Jane. Sure enough, she was making googly eyes right back at Henry. Like a fucking teenager.

Lolo crossed the kitchen in order to put her hand on Red's shoulder, to turn the woman's attention away from Henry, out the door, and on to her Mommy's Night Out drinks with her little friends, but the room was so small she knocked into Fat Jane before she made it to Red. "Fuck," Lolo said, "Sorry, momma." Before Manny was laid off, she'd had a nice kitchen with tile counters and enough room to make a Thanksgiving meal. It was a kitchen you could maneuver around without touching anyone, ever.

Fat Jane planted her hands, hands that were always touching her mouth, her nose, touching everything, on Lolo as if to steady herself. She was a dramatic woman. On more than one occasion, Lolo had seen her kiss her fingers and touch the bags she dropped off. "For the orphans," Fat Jane would say, her voice dropping at the end as she pressed her just kissed fingers to the bags while Henry unloaded them from her Igloo. She loved to use the word "orphan," saying it two or three times a visit in a quiet whisper, the way other people said "cancer." Now, she leaned in for a bear hug. "You're doing God's work," she said. Lolo tried her best to relax into the other woman's bosom, to not turn rigid or recoil from the embrace she already knew would linger too long. At least Fat Jane always smelled good, like expensive perfume applied lightly, a bit of jasmine on top of the smell of baby powder and Desitin that circled the room when the women came with their coolers.

"No, it is you three," Lolo said, finally wriggling free. "You are the ones donating. The ones doing His work."

Lolo slid out of the button-up she'd put on to meet with the Janes, leaving it splayed on the floor, still buttoned. Her arms itched from the fabric touching her, itched from Fat Jane touching her, itched from the breath of all the Janes touching her, from the way they all felt the need to lay a hand on her arm or shoulder or wrist as they said goodbye, the now empty Igloos swinging in their grips. Saint Lolo, patron of hungry, baby orphans everywhere. The tank top she wore underneath, like most of her others, was ripped, but she couldn't stand the idea of going out to the store to try on new ones, and she'd put on some weight, wasn't sure what size to order. She just kept wearing the ones she had.

"Manny, where'd you put the box from Amazon?" she called out, slipping her shoes off as Port danced around her feet. "And bring me those cut-offs on the bed, huh?" She took off her pants and Port snuggled into her pile of discarded clothes. "Now you love me," she said to the dog. The affected accent was gone, leaving only a bit of a drawl that just barely smudged and smeared the edges of her words. "Do you see them?" she said, once again raising her voice so Manny could hear her in the next room. "They might be on the floor there. Manny, are you listening to me? And look, tell Henry, I'll have these ready to take out to the freezer in a bit. I ain't waiting for him to save his game." The men had turned on the PlayStation the second the Janes disappeared.

"Henry can hear you. Everyone in the neighborhood can hear you, chica."

The breast milk that Henry'd emptied from the coolers was stacked in a messy pile in the fridge. She got all but three bags out. Each of the Janes used the same standing storage bags. Lolo'd shown the women where to buy them online the first time she had the group over, and they were very good about buying just what she asked. They were her best girls.

A nun from Saint Jerome's Children's Home would come pick up about a third of the bags that women like the Janes donated. The rest went with Manny and Henry to the weightlifters, football players, and wannabes they sold to in the parking lots and locker rooms of local gyms.

She found her life was easiest if she recruited pumpers in numbers, little groups of friends that shuffled in and out together, that saw each other's coolers, noticed each other's output. And she aimed for women just like the Janes. Pretty, middle class girls who searched for books about organic composting and baby sign language online. She found them through her tech support job. Everything was automated by a neat little program she coded. Whenever someone fit the shopping profile she set up and also lived within a hundred-mile radius, the program noticed. The data was shuffled along to a print on demand site and the woman was sent glossy pamphlets about the hungry orphans at Saint Jerome's. Manny had done a good job designing the brochures—clean lines, a fancy logo.

He was so good it broke her heart. He missed working. She knew it.

When a breastfeeding woman with more than enough milk to donate read Manny's pamphlet and, tears choking her as she imagined the hollow stomachs plaguing a clutch of motherless babes, called Lolo, Lolo encouraged her to connect with like-minded pals before setting up an informational get together. "The more the merrier," she'd say, her voice as bright as she could make it.

Manny dropped the cardboard box she'd asked for on the counter and kissed her. "You're going to feel like shit if something happens to Mama H after you've been telling people she's dead."

"I ain't said she was dead."

He popped her on the butt, just where the leg of her underwear cut her soft fat, and Lolo squeaked, happy to pretend to be silly and young. "All right, all right. I sort of did, but you have to admit it was funny."

He gave her another kiss and nodded. "There's more than enough milk in the back freezer to do a delivery," he said.

"This set will round out another case, plus some. You and Henry can circle around to the gyms with them tomorrow."

Writing the original program was just a distraction, a fun data mining project that stretched her mind better than what she did all day, suggesting customers turn computers off and on again when the company site locked up. Lolo liked doing back-end work, hated customers, actually, but they mostly gave those assignments to the guys who would—who could—go into the office. So she'd started mining data as a side project. The breast milk came later, after she heard one of Henry's jock friends brag about its benefits. He got it directly from the source, apparently, and claimed right boobs were better than lefts.

Lolo cut open the box and pulled out the bag of caffeine powder she'd ordered. Ten years ago, when she stopped leaving the house, their old house, their real house, shopping wasn't this easy. Manny had to do everything for them then, work, groceries, bills, everything. She pulled a couple of trays filled with plastic capped tubes from the cabinet. She ordered those online, too. Each held less than three ounces, a perfect shot for a big man, and was freezable. "Hey, where's my scale?" she said. She looked past Manny to the living room. "Damn it, Henry, do you have the scale?"

"Hold on," he called back. "Manny, you should see this shit. I'm killing it."

"Henry, I swear to God—No, asshole, I swear to the Virgin that if I have to come in there and take my fucking scale from you again I will put a knife through your pretty abs."

"Come get some, puta."

Manny made a show of rolling his eyes as Lolo pantomimed knifing the both of them. "You people need to calm your tits. It's ok, bro, I'll come get it," he said.

The caffeine had to be measured carefully. Lolo weighed each spoonful before whisking it into the milk. It took very little over the maximum dosage to do real damage, maybe even kill a person. And caffeine powder was bitter as hell. Putting a small enough amount in the milk so that the taste was masked while simultaneously getting in a large enough dose to give a little kick was a matter of precision and care, the key to convincing their clients breast milk did everything Manny and Henry and the internet message boards promised. Everything their little hearts desired. Make them stronger. Faster. Have more stamina. Increase muscle density. Cure fucking cancer. Walk on water. All without shrinking their balls. The caffeine powder provided the unexpected zing any skeptics needed. And it was cheap. And legal to buy.

The whole enterprise was basically legal. Mostly legal. And nearly 100 percent profit.

Lolo poured and capped, poured and capped until her little linoleum counter was covered in line after line of individually bottled breast milk shots. An army of money-making soldiers that would free her and Manny and Port from his brother's shitty little rental house and get them back to as near a normal life as Lolo could manage.

The headset Lolo wore to do customer support was too tight under her ear, prickling a pressure point, but it was the cheapest Bluetooth set she could find and it freed her to wander the yard with Port.

"Yes. Yes. Right. I will, absolutely. But I need you to tell me exactly what the error message says." Her cigarettes were a bit damp with morning dew and she imagined mold spores flecking the tobacco, blooming in her lungs, spreading like clover until she was a mess of fluffed-up white and green inside. "No, sir." With a little effort, she lit one anyway. "Yes, sir. But to help you I really need the exact message, sir." She closed her eyes and filled the air with smoke rings while the gentleman on the other end of the line yelled at her. She didn't watch them rise into the big empty sky, a thing to panic under, but enjoyed the act, the way the memory of learning to puff them out seemed to have settled into her muscles more than her mind.

She sat down next to Mary, pulled an oversized phone from her back pocket, and using her pinky, remoted into her computer and then into the customer's. "Ok, sir," she leaned her head against the statue's shoulder, "can you show me exactly what you were doing when the error message appeared?"

The sound of Manny's truck, coughing and grumbling out of gear, and then Port, coughing and grumbling into gear as he barked out his greeting, drowned out the beginning of the client's answer. But he was yelling again anyways, so Lolo just nodded her head against the folds of the Virgin's veil and smoked.

When the nun from Saint Jerome's knocked, her signature "shave and a haircut" pounding, Lolo had to answer the door. Henry was screwing Red Jane in the backroom and Manny was delivering a crate of breast shots to a high school coach with a big game on the horizon. It was the sort of situation that made Lolo itch. All of it was horrible.

The nun trying to make small talk.

Red Jane's grunting.

Port answering each and every guttural groan with a wheezing cough.

Lolo's own quick breaths as her anxiety mounted.

It was a symphony of horrible. And the fear that Red Jane would appear, half naked and sweaty, and see how just little of her milk the nun left with, would find out exactly what they were up to, was just icing on the shit cake.

This was Manny's job, this nun stuff, and Lolo scratched red grooves in her arms until the nun was gone, swinging two grocery bags of frozen breast milk and cold packs out the door and to the children's home. At least she hadn't been wearing a wimple.

Lolo hid in the yard, leaning against the Virgin until Red Jane was also gone and Manny was home. "I hate him," she said to Manny as he rubbed his hands over the welts on her arms.

"I know. But he loves you. He loves me. He loves Port. And, besides, you hate everyone." He pinched her side to make her laugh and Lolo did, happy to at least pretend.

Since the nun, she'd mostly hidden in the bedroom, the rest of the house feeling less hers than usual. Even the kitchen was lost to her. A strange space. She left anything she couldn't take care of from the bed to the boys.

"I need you to turn on desktop sharing," Lolo said. She picked a thread from the bedspread and tried to imagine a face for the man on the other end of the call. But she wasn't good with faces, even in her imagination. "There should be a little square you can check, mm hmmm, uh huh. Sir? Sir? Sir, is your computer on?"

She could hear Henry banging around in the kitchen. Messing up all of her careful order. Her fridge, her freezer, she knew they would be a jumbled mess now.

The boys were just not clean and careful like she was. She had to do everything.

A woman's voice climbed over the clamor occasionally. Lolo slid under the covers.

And though she still slipped outside with Port in the early mornings, keeping her eyes low so she could imagine the little fence line stretched high enough to keep her safe from the outside world, the trips were getting shorter, her imagination filling the tight yard with a misty sense of danger.

The sun had barely crested the fence the morning Henry came running out of the house so fast that Lolo ducked, terrified he was going to bowl her over.

She had, by now, stopped going farther from the house then the first tree, a fat, old Sawtooth Oak she thought of as home base. She had Manny move The Virgin under its thick branches. Ducking Henry sent her nearly out of its shadow. Dangerously so.

Her throat felt tight.

She pressed the mute button next to her ear. "What are you doing awake?" She knew it sounded like, "I hate you," but couldn't stop herself. He'd ruined it. Ruined the last bit of outside and now she was trapped in it, him between her and the door.

"Chel took the wrong milk," he said.

"What?"

"She isn't answering her cell."

"Who?" Lolo un-pressed the mute button. "Sir, I think we are having connectivity issues. I can't quite hear—" She tapped the button twice more, cutting herself off and hanging up the phone. Removed the headset. "Who took what wrong milk?" Even in the sheltered shadow of the tree, she could feel the delicious, calming heat of the sun breaking through the branches. Instead of looking up to catch sight of the shifting light, she tried to follow its movements in the shadows on the ground behind Henry.

He put his hand over his face. "Late last night, we had some champagne to celebrate her divorce papers. You know how she is, she didn't want to risk any of it—"

"Who is?"

"Chel. She was going to pump and dump once she got home, but needed some milk for this morning's feeding in case her ex used all she left with him. I told her to grab some from the fridge."

Confused, Lolo just looked at Henry.

"God dammit, niña, listen. Chel. My girlfriend. Two months. Red hair. How the fuck do you not know this?"

Lolo brushed her nails across her skin. She had no answer. But she understood now.

Red. She took the wrong milk. To her infant.

She wanted to leave the yard. To get back in the house. Her bedroom. She wanted to lie down and nap until Manny got home. She wanted to switch the direction of the conversation away from her, what she missed, wanted to chastise him for being careless. Why was the caffeinated milk in the front fridge to begin with, she wanted to say, why the fuck hadn't he put everything in its place, used her neat, clean layout, her careful rows? But the panic on his face stopped her. "Are you sure? Are you a hundred percent positive?"

"I don't know. Yes. Probably. Maybe." Lolo could hear Henry's teeth clattering together as he thought, a habit he'd had for as long as she'd known him. "I don't know. You told us not to store them next to each other. You were, you know, sleeping a lot, and it just seemed faster. I can't—"

This wasn't her fault.

How could she have known? Lolo shifted down into the grass and said the words silently. *Not my fault.* "Okay. You have to get her. It's that simple. You and Manny. You have to go get her before she feeds the baby. How old is it?"

Manny. She needed Manny.

"Six months. And I can't go. Manny has the truck. He's out getting groceries."

"You have to call her."

"I told you—"

Lolo hid her shaking hands. "Then call him." Why wasn't he here with her?

When she still watched TV, she'd liked cop shows, nature shows, mysteries, documentaries. They'd watched a lot together, on the couch, bodies touching easily, no work to it.

Even as she slowly stopped leaving the house, at first just afraid to drive, then to ride, then to be in crowded places, then in open places, in those first couple of years she'd let the outside world in through her television. But finally, that stopped, too. She'd been very careful to keep everything out. Keep herself safe. Sharks, drownings, dengue, murderers, parasites, falling, fires, crowds, heights, careening accidents, collapsing buildings—she'd spent ten years imagining every possible dangerous, terrifying thing. Real things, fake things. She'd taken up less and less space. They both had.

"He isn't picking up."

In all these years, Lolo'd never once imagined she was the danger. The thing someone else would need protecting from.

"Call 911," she said. "If you can't get Red—Chel—if you really can't get her, we have to call 911."

Nothing they'd done had been legal. No matter what she told herself, what she told Manny, what she whispered to the Mary on her smoke breaks, it hadn't been. And it was all her idea. Her fault.

She could not stand anymore. Sat in the grass in front of the Virgin. Leaned her head as far back as it would go, the concrete behind her a comforting stop, and tried to open her eyes. She tried to force herself to look into the dizzying blue above.

Without changing position, she pressed the keys on her handset. She didn't need to look to find them.

"What's your emergency?"

She wanted to say, "I need Manny," but of course she didn't. That would be insane. She tried to concentrate on the baby. That she'd hurt the baby if she didn't speak. That suddenly she was filled with horrible power. But it was hard. She pressed her head further back, so a sharp edge in the statue's concrete grated against her scalp and wondered what prison would be like. Everything dirty. Everything touching.

Alone. And never alone.

Lolo strained to hear the truck, to hear Port greeting her husband. As if she could will Manny into being the way she tried to will the rest of the world away.

Her closed lids burned orange, and as she found the words, Lolo imagined falling upward, disappearing into the overwhelming space she knew was there waiting.

Ghosts

It was Sunday. Viv'd wasted their only day off together, the day she and Corrie normally walked or shopped or tested out new recipes Corrie found on the web. Their only all-day day together. She wouldn't leave the bed. She wouldn't dress. She wouldn't eat. A triangle of sunlight crawled across the comforter, growing narrow and long, until finally a bit of moonlight, a muted glow, replaced it. This was Sunday. Not *a* Sunday, but *the* Sunday, the day her mother left when she was ten. Killed herself. Corrie joined her, curling her lithe body next to her on and off. She'd place her hand on Viv's bare stomach and talk to her, maybe switch on the stereo, tell a dirty joke, ask if she'd read this bit or that bit of news, then she'd get up and make sandwiches that Viv would just ignore or run out for Cokes that Viv would not drink.

Viv always celebrated this way, drunk and melodramatic, suffering, perhaps terminally this time, from a case of what her mother liked to call the *petit malaise* and her father called *comiendo mierda,* eating shit.

Together three years and it was only the second time she'd done this in front of Corrie, been this naked and full broken version of herself, and Corrie didn't tell her she was ridiculous, excessive. Indulgent. She didn't push her to put on clothes. Instead, she balanced a tomato sandwich on Viv's breast and, tilting it this way and that with her little finger, the sandwich an obscene seesaw, said, "How about we get us a little baby?" Viv knew she was trying to make her smile, her own grin big and infectious and waiting.

She had strong, white teeth Viv loved and so she gave in, laughing at this piece of silliness and closing the book she wasn't reading, dropping it to the floor. "I love your hands."

"She would take after you, freckles, light eyes. We could call her Princess Mopes-A-Lot."

A game. "No, your eyes. Dark eyes." Viv dangled her pinky in her glass of bourbon and branch, stirred it. An absurd gesture, she knew. Theatrical. But then she smiled for Corrie, a real one, small and tight, but real. Still, she couldn't help jutting her chin a little to look thinner, smoother there. "So, royalty?"

"Sure. Our kids'll rule the ghosts."

It was an old joke between them, born of the way they both floated around, the two of them self-proclaimed half-breeds, not belonging. Not anchored. American ghosts. It was a bit they'd built over the years. Short hand jokes.

They shared a common vocabulary.

"A baby," Viv said, imagining how that would fix everything. She propped herself up and took a sip from her drink. "Something just ours." Someone to belong to.

On their third date, Viv had decided to cook for Corrie. She almost made it through the evening without incident. Then, she made coffee. She miss-threaded the top of her old-fashioned stovetop espresso maker, and as the water boiled, it began spraying liquid from its middle. Mahogany fluid and her white sundress coming together in all the glory of a Jackson Pollock. She swore in English, French, Spanish, Vietnamese, and Italian. She swore in sign language and with international gestures. It went on too long. Was ridiculous. Drama fit for a telenovela.

"Wow," Corrie said. "Wow."

She stood there ashamed, wanting to cry. Begging herself to not cry. Thinking this is how it ends. How she scares this tall, muscular thing, this beautiful woman so different from herself right out of her life.

"You're quite the polyglot."

Then Viv laughed and Corrie looked at her the way she had always wanted someone to, like she was startling and wonderful. "Nah, I just speak a little pidgin. You?"

"Indians only speak pidgin in the movies."

It was on that third date that she fell. Tumbled. Knew Corrie was it.

She told her about her mother that perfect night, sort of. The two of them on her couch, Viv's feet tucked under Corrie's thighs to keep her toes warm. She told her about Paris and Havana. "They came to America to have a baby, I guess. Then they went home."

"I thought your father still lived in Miami," Corrie said, her head in Viv's lap, Viv's hands gently pulling her long hair into a loose braid.

"Sure. Miami." She loved the way her skin looked against Corrie's, both of them yellow. "Tell me about your family."

"My dad works offshore. My mom teaches accordion." Viv noticed faint wrinkles darting from the center of Corrie's eyes down nearly to her cheekbones.

"You were born in Elton?"

"Nah. They just live there now. My dad worked on a boat when I was a kid. We lived in Natchez." Her eyes closed.

"You been there, to the reservation out that way?"

"Sure. There's this pow wow every year. I go. I don't love it, but I see my grandma. My cousins." Her voice drifted. "It's huge."

Viv listened to her breath slowing, thickening. "It must be nice," she said, once she knew Corrie was asleep. She had run from her own family early and she missed them, the big dinners, the noise. They had been nothing but good to her and she ran away. Like her mother.

Viv was seven months pregnant, their second try, when she finally met the old woman, Síhnosi. Corrie's grandmother had filled Viv's imagination for years, but she'd never accompanied Corrie on visits. "You know I don't do family," she'd say whenever Corrie pulled out the suitcase and patted the space she'd leave in it for Viv's things. But, late last week, Corrie's father had not woken up from his afternoon nap and Viv had been the one to pull out the suitcase. On the drive to Elton, she asked, "Will she like me?"

Corrie laughed. She had this great horsey laugh normally, but now it was flat, more breath than bray. "No. She hates everyone." Viv was not sure if she was being teased. They turned down a gravel road lined by thin, piney forest. "Babe, my dad was her baby. I wouldn't expect much."

Viv looked out the window. "Of course." She knew she should be comforting Corrie, not the other way around. Still, she whined a little more and Corrie touched the tips of her fingers to her leg, laid them there on her knee and drove with the other hand, but she was silent for the rest of the ride. Viv kept her eyes on the passing trees, her hand on the curve of her belly. She fell asleep like that, eyes turned toward the window, palm against the baby within, not waking until the car rolled to a stop. The house was small and beige with a neat lawn. Next to it sat its twin, and a triplet beyond. They all looked relatively new, and Viv saw horses in the field across the street. It was not at all what she expected. But she hadn't really known what to expect.

Corrie opened Viv's door, but she sat still. "You can't stay in there all day. Come on."

The truth was Viv didn't want to meet the grandmother. She didn't want to meet the cousins, the aunts, or the uncles. She wanted to go home. It had been her idea, but still she fretted. "Maybe I could wait in the car." Corrie just looked at her. "Please," she said rubbing her belly like a lamp. "Please."

Corrie pulled her up and kissed her, right there in the driveway, and whispered, "Come on," into Viv's cheek, her mouth leaving a bit of wet there so Viv could still feel her lips as they walked in.

The inside of the house was small, tidy, and the beige kitchen was barely an offshoot from the living area. The smell of pine was everywhere, not supermarket air freshener, but real needles. The grandmother stood at a thick table that seemed too close to the stove, her strong, angular hands working dough in a wooden bowl. There were intricately woven baskets in a variety of sizes decorating every shelf in the room. Some were shaped like animals, frogs or ducks, others were decorated with pinecones or fruit.

"Síhnosi." Corrie moved towards her grandmother, but the old woman held up her hands. They were gnarled and covered in flour.

"Sit," she said, looking at Viv. "Your mother's sleeping." Her drawl was clipped by another, softer accent, the Lost Tribe's, Viv thought, the words conjuring drama. Corrie'd explained it was what people called them, the Lost Tribe. When Viv said it was romantic, Corrie had laughed. "Not hardly," she'd said.

Síhnosi, put her hands back in the bowl, "She's cut all her hair off."

Still drowsy and living in the intermittent fog her obstetrician blamed on the pregnancy, Viv was confused. Mamman? She'd had a bad dream in the car. The sad drive to see Corrie's family leaving her thinking of her own.

"I figured," Corrie said, laying a hand on her shoulder. "Síhnosi this is Viv, my—" and then that awkward pause she did sometimes when introducing Viv.

Partner, Viv said silently. Love, she willed Corrie to say. Girlfriend, she begged her to finish. But Corrie just left it there.

"Wife," Síhnosi said with a little sigh on the F that Viv only later learned was from emphysema, nothing more. "Your mother showed me the pictures you sent."

They'd had a commitment ceremony, a small party but still grand, with drinks and balloons and Elvis officiating, before the first in vitro treatment, the one that didn't take. The second was the miscarriage. Her mind felt trapped in the past. Not letting her loose.

"That wasn't a very good Elvis, no?" Síhnosi said.

"No." Viv's mother had loved the King, would have hated the funny little man that wore an ill-fitting version of his jumpsuit to their wedding. "Cherie, that man can move," she'd say every time Elvis came on the radio. Then she'd wiggle her hips, and Viv's dad would laugh. At ten, Viv found her floating in the tub, the water pink from her opened wrists, her hair slithering around pale hips. "Are You Lonesome Tonight" playing in the background.

For a second she imagined she felt her, her mother, right here in this old woman's kitchen, smelled the violet water she'd smoothed over both their scalps every morning, every night, every time it was hot. When Viv was little, Mamman would get Viv's grandmother, her husband's mother, to ship it from Miami. Always angry about what she couldn't buy after they moved to Louisiana.

Viv saw it in the drugstores now, but would not pick it up. Did not want the smell.

She pulled at a lock of her own hair, tried to untangle Síhnosi's words from memories. But she just kept thinking of her mother's hair, red and wavy. She wished the baby might have the same fire top, but they'd used Corrie's egg and her womb, a stranger's sperm. Corrie not wanting to carry a child, her work offshore too physically demanding. So that hair, it was gone forever.

"Why?" Viv said, not sure of what she was asking.

"He was fat." The woman plunged her hands back into the dough. It was the only thing she said to Viv the whole day.

They moved to be closer to Corrie's family, Corrie arguing that it would make life easier, better. Viv missed her friends, but she liked Elton, even if she felt like an outsider. And Corrie's family was a good one to be just outside of. Bubbling with life.

When she had the baby, they brought him to Síhnosi's house, and he squealed until they opened the door. Then, in that small, brown home, he stopped. She noticed nearly all the little cousins were like that, raucous outside the door, rolling all over Viv at the family barbeques, squealing and bobbing for attention, then fairly quiet as they hit Síhnosi's threshold.

"You hear that, babe?" Corrie said.

Viv heard it and blessed it. She hadn't slept in weeks. Corrie was offshore so much right now, having scored a full time job as a geologist for an oil company that she used to just contract for. Practically the only woman on the rig not cooking or cleaning. Viv was so proud, but that baby, he cried. "You think we could leave Bobby here?" she said. "Just drop him on the couch, bundled up with a note, and run?"

Corrie laughed, the old horsey laugh. It had showed up again with Bobby. "Don't worry, babe, we'll get you a nurse soon." Viv's father'd sent money and attached a note both cryptic and clear. "For help," it said, and Viv knew that he'd thought of her mother, so often *sick* after her birth. "Send pictures," it said. But Viv hadn't.

Síhnosi pulled the baby from her arms, rumpled his thick black crown. "A nurse? You sick?"

"She's just tired," Corrie said. She always said *nurse*, not *nanny*, not *help*. Ashamed, Viv thought. None of Corrie's family would ever imagine hiring a nanny. The cost alone was an embarrassment.

They followed Síhnosi into the kitchen. A mortar and pestle sat on the table. "Soup?" Corrie asked, nudging a chair back with her hip.

Viv wondered at the quietness of the adults in this family, at the way her girl, usually so talkative, slipped out of words when she came here.

"Tomorrow." Síhnosi puckered her lips, and they cracked into a star burst of lines. She touched the baby's forehead. "He's a strong one. A wrestler like his grandda?"

"Damn near pulled my hair out by the roots last night," she said, wishing for a beer. She was breastfeeding all the time it seemed like. Bobby so needy.

"Why don't your people come and help you?" Síhnosi asked, eyes never off the baby.

"Ghosts," Viv answered.

It was years ago, at TéTe's pub in Natchez, the both of them silly with tequila, when they came up with the idea of the Ghost Culture. It was before Bobby came, before they were even *really* officially official. They'd fallen into a discussion of the way people loved to ask what you *are*. Everyone so curious about your sex life, your skin, your people.

"I don't know where in France she was from," Viv said, dropping peanut shells onto the floor. Her mother would have hated the mess at TeTe's. Loved the music. The way all the women danced with abandon. Free of the outside world, which could not peek in the shuttered windows. "And she never writes," Viv said, adoring her own little joke. She hadn't yet told Corrie her mother was dead. Just said she was gone.

"Shit. I know plenty." Corrie said, "I know I got this big-assed nose from my Dad, and I know how to dance. I can even do the hustle. Mom taught me." She wiggled a little. "Doesn't help."

Viv tipped glass to lip. "I know Marsha Brady, and I know to always give my answer in the form of a question." They went on like that for a while, taking breaks from their little joke to dance, to order drinks, to pee.

"I know," Corrie paused, solemnly raised her hand, palm out like a movie Indian, America's joke, and said stoically, "How." Then she laughed. "What, Where, When, and Why." Then she was quite again. "That Hollywood shit pisses me off. Make people sound like idiots."

"Man, someone asks me what I am," Viv rubbed her skin, pulling at its color, not dark, not light, "I say nothing. I ain't a part of nothing."

Corrie leaned over and kissed her nose. "You pretty white chick."

"Seriously, chica."

"Seriously? You're a part of America's great Ghost Culture. All of us thinking about some dead people like they tell us who we are. Or worse, pretend people on the television. All us a part of something not quite solid." Corrie ran her hand over Viv's, the friction making her skin hot, making Viv's eyes land on her collar bone, the rise of breast under it. "You know it's there, but you can't quite see it."

"Dead and haunting?" Viv asked, leaning closer to Corrie, trying to forget the way the idea made her think of her mother, trying to banish a sadness that suddenly creeped up, trying to take Corrie in, instead. Her smell. Her heat. Her words. Trying to make it just the two of them in that big, full bar.

"Something like that," then Corrie kissed her hard enough that Viv shivered at the way her lips would be tomorrow, bruised and full. "Now, seriously, my place?"

Síhnosi never left Viv alone about her family once she guessed something was wrong. Always asking those short questions of hers. "Your mother, she's Cajun? She makes gumbo, has a good recipe?"

"She's French." Viv nudged her nipple into the baby's searching mouth. She'd started coming to Síhnosi's house whenever Corrie was working. She missed her so much. Was sad all the time. She told herself it was the silences she came for. The way they stretched on for hours here. The way the baby somehow respected them. But she also came to be next to the heat of another adult. Bobby's small heat not enough for her.

And it wasn't really silent here, anyway. That was just a myth she liked, as if this was a magic place instead of a mundane kitchen. Síhnosi would chatter on the phone with friends for hours if she wasn't busy. She liked the radio, too. Kept it going. The place was alive, not a shrine. But it was a different kind of quiet than Viv's own quiet home, filled just with the noises she and the baby made at each other, at themselves, whenever Corrie was away.

Síhnosi went back to her weaving, humming deep in her throat as she worked. Not quite in tune with the radio, not quite out of tune. An hour later, she said, as if no time at all had passed, "Your mother's coming to the ceremony?"

At four months, the family was supposed to gather around Bobby while an uncle shaved his head, leaving it clean and new. "What is with you people and hair?" Viv said, irritated. You people. The words gross in her mouth.

"To cut the hair is a cleansing. And a letting go." Síhnosi touched her own gray hair, which fell past her shoulders in frizzy waves. "The ceremony for Bobby is about his future. All our futures. It's about hope."

Viv did not want to shave Booby's hair. It was dark and stick straight like Corrie's. A thing to love. "And Corrie's mom? Her hair?"

"That was just a different kind of hope." The old woman started humming again, and Viv put Bobby in the bassinet Síhnosi'd set up for her in the kitchen.

"She's not coming." Viv said, feeling lost in this family that knew itself so well. She'd never told any of them about her mother, and Corrie hadn't either. "Your business," she would say.

Síhnosi just hummed along with the radio.

Viv rocked Bobby.

The year Mamman died, she'd shorn Viv's hair off. "What was France like?" Viv'd asked for the hundredth time, as her mother brushed her knots out—a thousand strokes every night.

"It was like Havana I expect, cherie. Be still."

"And what was Havana like?" Viv looked to her father.

Her mother jerked her head back. "Be still, I said."

"It was green, and there was dancing."

"Well, Paris certainly wasn't green, but other parts, oui. And dancing, of course." Her mother's hand was not gentle that night, and Viv started to cry. "Cherie, hush. It hurts to be beautiful, you know."

Her father looked up from his paper. "Be a good girl, Viv, and I'll take you to the calle tomorrow. We can go to the trick shop."

Viv smiled, and her mother jerked her head again. "Be still."

"Have a little patience, Marie."

"Merde." Her mother popped Viv in the back of the head with the brush. "I am sick of it. Sick to death. Do something with your daughter, Carlos. I'm not having a wild child in this house." Viv's mother's voice had risen to a pitch that Viv knew to be frightened of. "I mean it, Carlos. Get me the ciseaux. If she can't keep it straight, I'll cut it."

The boys at school laughed the next day when they saw her ruined head.

So Viv hated the idea of cutting Bobby's hair, but she didn't tell the old women that. Instead she just hummed with her and watched the light in the kitchen shift.

Finally, Síhnosi spooned a heavy portion of hominy soup into Viv's bowl. "She could fly in for the ceremony, no?"

Viv didn't answer. They ate in silence. "Could you teach me to weave?" she said instead of all the other things she wanted to.

Viv was on her way to Síhnosi's house for the ceremony when the accident happened. It was before sunrise, and Bobby'd cried all night. Corrie was offshore. A storm—one not bad enough to fly the helicopters out for, but too bad to run the boats in—was keeping her away. So Viv drove the old Chevy down that gravel road by herself, and when she dozed off, it slammed into the pines. Somehow, she pulled Bobby from his seat before passing out.

The heat of the flames woke her. The smell of tires on fire burned even worse than the smoke in her eyes.

Strangers found her screaming, the skin burnt from her hands, her shoulder. Her child in her ruined arms.

On the morphine, Viv dreamed her hair was very long, filled with knots, and that somewhere in it was Bobby. She could hear him crying, but she couldn't find him. She pulled and pulled, but there was just more hair there. She looked over and saw Síhnosi.

"Not fit for weaving," the old woman said, weaving her own gray locks into a tidy basket. "Not fit for anything."

When Viv woke in the hospital, Síhnosi was there.

"Corrie is coming, no fears," she said, watching Viv carefully. There was a half-finished basket on her lap, and her hands moved swiftly over it. A bag of pine needles sat on the chair next to her.

"Bobby?"

Síhnosi looked at the cell phone clutched in her hand. "Corrie is on her way," she said again. "Sleep."

Viv was not sure when exactly Corrie arrived, painkillers destroyed her sense of time and left her feeling detached, disconnected anytime she woke up. But when Corrie appeared, her face was completely still, like her grandmother's. Only, Viv could see how careful she was being not to move any of it, how new and strange this stillness was for her. She looked like a mannequin or a chiseled bit of stone.

"I fell asleep," Viv said. Her voice flat, nothing in it. Something inside growled at her. Scream, it said. Cry. But she just laid there.

"He's fighting." Corrie touched her hand. Viv's bandages looked strangely white, an unexpected break between the rich colors of their skin. She laid her head against Viv's chest, and Viv, resting her chin against the softness of Corrie's hair, felt the breast of her gown grow damp as Corrie's body shook against her, rattling her own.

And she desperately wanted to find the frequency of her grief, to shake against Corrie. But she couldn't.

Any time Corrie left, Viv awoke to find Síhnosi watching her, and when Síhnosi disappeared, Corrie took her place. Bobby was one floor up, maybe dying, but they did not wheel Viv to see him. She was also maybe dying. An infection in the burns that would not let her hold him.

When the bandages came off, Corrie was with the baby who had healed faster than Viv had. A strange blessing. Viv told the doctors to let her be, and she watched a dapple of sunlight play against the wall as they snipped and pulled and stripped away the gauze. Once they were gone, she asked Síhnosi for the pair of scissors she kept in her bag. She placed them on the bed tray, next to a cup of applesauce. Viv pulled her auburn hair free of the hospital gown, the edges ragged and curled from heat, chunks missing where the doctors hacked it away from her wounds. Strands stayed knotted in the tie at the base of her neck, but she didn't pull at them. "Here," she said, turning to the wall to give Síhnosi easy access to her hair.

"No," she said and gestured to Viv's hands. "You. This is your decision. Your ritual. Your prayer."

It took a while for her to get her mottled fingers, tight and clumsy now, through the loops in the handles. She started cutting and didn't stop until the white of the hospital bed was littered with her auburn waves and some of the ghosts were gone.

At the Very End

The cigarette is very, very small in Uncle's hands, the burning ash a bright bit of fairy-light in the afternoon gloom. He is the biggest man in the family. Biggest in the Parish and maybe all Louisiana. But not the biggest in the world. That one is in Turkey, and he beats Uncle by less than half a foot.

We are in a farm graveyard, with simple aboveground slabs decorated with plastic flowers tipped by shifting winds. The plots are too small for Uncle. They are more my size. Which is good.

It is the sort of private cemetery you find in rural areas. The road we followed was just gravel and then was not at road at all, only ruts. Shallow earth peppered with grass shoots. The farm land that surrounds us is grown over, given to goats and thin cattle.

"It's quiet," he says and I nod.

It would be stupid to think this place is empty, that the broken trailers sinking into soft mud across the way are abandoned. Where there is land, there are people.

But no one peeks out of bent doorframes to see what we want.

I'm small the way Uncle is big. And I'm dying.

Not tonight. Not here with Uncle in this graveyard in front of these poor farmlands and bleating goats. But soon enough.

Uncle puts his hand on my face, and it is as if I am a moon in a fairytale, cupped by a giant, playing at making a sky. I watch the brilliant ashes teeter in his other hand.

I climb on one of the slabs. There are trees to see and buttercups and rusted farm supplies. I've wanted this sort of aboveground grave, this simple slab, for as long as I've known. Wanted to forever in a field like this, instead of the big church cemetery my mother bought a plot in.

"Here," I say, more powerful than I have felt in my whole life.

And Uncle, the only one that understands, nods. Looks for a door to knock on. A person to make a deal with.

Pinched Magnolias

Dalia brought the butt of her shotgun to her shoulder. Everything was damp, clammy, and the air smelled of blooming magnolias and churned up swamp bed, sweet and earthy all at once. Her husband stood, grinning, on the edge of her property where water met land. He spread his arms, palms towards God, and shrugged a little. Bud was a large man, wide and tall, and his broad shoulders looked ridiculous shuffling around under his denim coveralls. He took a step forward, his mudboots sinking into the black gumbo of the bayou that banked her garden.

"Off my yard, Bud. Now," she said, like she might have said, "Pick up that mess." Tired sounding, mostly. Bud took another little step, his open arms easing down, and Dalia wriggled her big toe around in the ground, digging a hole. Otherwise, she was still, a five-foot statue in a wide hat and flower print dress. Her voice was steady and calm, her anger only apparent in how heavy her drawl had become. "Get back, I said."

Like most of the women in Marti Parish, she'd been brought up with one finger on a trigger, and the weight of the gun felt good in her hands, natural. But Bud was the sort of fool who figured she wouldn't use it, and he kept walking. "Baby, give me that big ol' gun," he said, that grin a smear across his face. "You know you ain't going to shoot nobody." It was the same tone he'd taken the first time he'd lifted her shirt in high school, the both of them grinning back then.

"Anybody. It's ANYbody, you asshole." She looked down at the hole she'd made in the soil. Her father'd had his own proverbs, wisdoms only he knew. "Nothing good ever grew from shotgun shells," he'd say, his arms often in the dirt, "but the brass gives roses color." The hole would do. "Take another step, Bud, really."

"Baby, you know I love you." His boots sucked at the ground.

Dalia pulled the trigger, smiled at Bud looking so damn surprised. "Fuck off," she said, the sweetness of her drawl hanging on the words. She nudged the dispensed shell with her foot and sunk it deep into the dirt, pushing it into her little hole until it all but disappeared. She finished covering it, her foot sweeping and smoothing the moist earth. Only then did she look over at her husband's body, at the ragged hole the buckshot had ripped through his chest, at the way the blood looked black as it pooled in the mud. She did a mimic of his little shrug and went inside the house to make a pot of coffee.

It wasn't that she didn't believe Bud loved her. Honestly, he was the sort of dumb mutt that loved everyone, therein lay the problem. She'd thrown him out when she realized that he was cheating on her, but like the old cur he was, he padded on back whenever he was hungry or lonely. He'd come in his boat, pulling in next to her daddy's old one, a peace offering of fresh-caught white perch and a half-drained six pack in his worn hands.

Even that, she could live with, but he wasn't secret with his whore. She'd eventually met the girl at the Piggly Wiggly, the both of them in the parking lot, Dalia's cart full of half a month's groceries, the girl's holding only gin and tampons. She was a little bit, short and dark like Dalia, maybe eighteen, dumb like him, and built like a rolling river, waves of her spilling out of her baby blue hot pants.

Still, Dalia could stomach it. Barely, but she could.

The girl was a stripper, of course, across the river at Pinky's, somehow managing not to get tetanus or typhus as she crossed its parking lot-slash-junk yard. Dalia knew the girl was just a symbol of everything that was wrong with Bud and his world and this town and had somehow managed not to hate the child whore. Not really.

She picked up her cell phone and watched the coffee drip. Her sister was sheriff, like their father had been, and was the only one to call.

"Mary," she said, the phone resting between ear and arm as she filled a little blue pitcher with cream and pulled out some china, "I've shot Bud. You might want to come."

After their father's death, Mary had let Dalia keep the family home but had stayed close. Three acres down, she was Dalia's nearest neighbor. On the other side, a few empty hunting camps leaned towards the ground, the timber heavy with humidity and neglect. Tangled woods choked with brush and dewberries stumbled around everything, slipping through and behind the sprawling lots. Only a gravel road and the bayou connected the homes, and in the thick of spring, even they seemed to get lost in the overgrowth.

The coffee pot was hot and ready when Mary stepped into the kitchen. Without even a hello, Dalia poured her a cup, and they sat at the table. Keeping her gaze on the pitcher and off of Dalia, Mary began spooning sugar into her cup.

Like so many sisters, they were opposites and made for mismatched bookends. Mary was slim and tall, her daddy's girl, and wore rumpled jeans and a t-shirt. Her black boots, so normal everywhere else, looked out of place and clunky across from her sister's small, naked feet. "Looks pretty bad out there," Mary said, finally making eye contact. "The flies are gathering."

"I'd expect. It's at least ninety."

"Really, D," Mary sounding sad now, "What on earth possessed you to shoot Bud?"

"He kept walking."

Mary let the spoon clink against the glass as she stirred and stirred. Finally, she just said, "They always do."

No one was surprised when Mary'd run for sheriff, Dalia sitting right behind her at every little speech. Marti was a small parish, and everyone had known and loved their daddy. He was good people, maybe not the most honest sheriff, but wasn't that the way. Honest and effective need not go together, not in Louisiana, and everyone understood Mary's need to avenge her father's murder, unsolved and itching at them all like a wound. She won easily enough, despite being a woman, her black hair yanked into a tight ponytail, skin scrubbed clean of any makeup, and Dalia behind her, bowing her head under the brim of a hat, touching her face with a tissue at the mention of their dad.

Dalia gave Mary a quick hug after she was sworn in and said, "He'd be proud," her voice not quite happy. Mary'd just nodded.

She'd turned out to be a good sheriff and had been reelected, her sister once again sitting behind her, giving her the rare hug.

The women stood in the yard looking down at Bud.

Mary said, "You should wear shoes out here," and Dalia wondered if she was just used to bossing people these days. "Stickers and snakes."

Dalia poking the body with her toe, "He was handsome when we met, sort of."

"He was. But now, well, it's a wonder he caught that girl's eye."

"Fairly certain he looked a bit better alive, drunk, and shoving dollars in her panties." Dalia chewed at her lip. "Idiot. He could make a girl feel special, though, loved. In his own way, I mean. And he was funny." The hem of her dress slipped into a mix of blood and dirt as she bent to look at her husband. She absently knotted the ends like when she was gardening. "But, dumb." She looked from Bud to Mary. "You know his girl looks like I did when I was young. Well, sluttier, but scrub her face and put some clothes on her…"

Her sister shook her head. "You ain't exactly old."

Dalia'd had enough of looking at Bud. Water lapped at the edge of the bank, eating it away, and she concentrated on that motion. Once upon a time when the sisters were barely more than babies, before their daddy'd told them that their mother'd run off, before they'd forgotten her smell, her voice, there had been a couple of more feet of land to play on out there, their little bodies getting bronze in the sun as they made mud pies. Their daddy drinking Beam and pretending to watch for gators as they played.

"This isn't okay," Mary said.

"No."

There was a rumble of tires against gravel and both women's heads shot up. Dalia could see a hint of black shifting behind the trees near the road. A pickup. She opened her mouth a little, finding it harder to breathe.

Mary closed her eyes, and Dalia listened to the soft shoosh of her breath. They waited. The car kept rolling. "That camp past my house, I think. That Dutch guy," Mary said, "It's got to be him."

"Shit." The sound of the tires was almost gone now.

"Just grab his feet," Mary said finally, waving a callused hand toward the back of the house.

Near the farthest corner of the property stood a wooden T-frame attached to an old metal shed, a winch and rope rigged to it. The nearest real grocery was the Piggly Wiggly forty-five minutes away, and so, like most everyone else they knew, the girls had been hunting for dinner since they could hold the weight of a Remington .410 steady. After a hunt, they had never been allowed to skip the skinning. "Real meat don't come in plastic wrap," their daddy'd said, slipping a noose high around the neck of a deer before cranking the winch. Once the carcass was dangling from the T-frame, hooves a good foot from the ground, he'd grab a hose, nod toward the knives, and say, "Watch how deep you cut. You bust the gut, you contaminate dinner." Then, his girls, not quite tall enough to work a good sized buck, would scrabble onto upturned pails. Their daddy, tall and lean, adding his muscle to the job when necessary.

All the buckets were right side up now, but the winch was still oiled and functioning. When hunting season came around in the fall, Mary'd bring what she bagged to her sister's house, dress it, and leave some of the meat in her freezer.

They half carried, half dragged Bud towards the T-frame.

"Jesus, D, the least you could do is keep your end up," Mary said.

Dalia's hat fell off as she tried to adjust her grip. They'd slipped Bud's boots off so she could get a good hold on his ankles, but they were wide and he was heavy, and the difference in the sisters' heights didn't make carrying him any easier. "Hold on," she said.

"No. We're almost there, and I certainly don't have all day. Buck the hell up." It was her father talking. Mary's mouth was moving, but Dalia knew that voice. She didn't answer, but she stopped and dropped Bud's feet, made a show of wiping the sweat from her face with the edge of her skirt despite its filth. Made a show of inspecting her hat, putting it firmly back on. Mary watched her, hands still looped under Bud's arms, making no move to clear her own eyes of sweat.

They traveled the last few feet without much noise, but when they got to the T-frame, Mary said, "This really isn't okay," and as they stripped the man, made the noose, turned the winch, Dalia wondered who in the hell she was talking to, which one of them she was trying to convince.

There is a myth that any meat dumped in the swamp will be eaten by gators, but a body dumped in the bayou was as like as not to end up floating into someone's camp. That's how the girls had found their daddy: his body bloated and nibbled but mostly intact, except for a missing finger or toe and that hole in his head that really only left his jaw in place.

That day Mary'd called the deputy, while Dalia, home from college, sat with the remains at the edge of the water, rocks and roots digging at her. Laying her fingers on his hand—the meat of it sloughed of skin in places—she'd cried a bit and hadn't returned to campus after, to take care of Mary, she told her friends.

So, the girls knew better than to put a whole man in the water.

They worked quickly, looking up every time a squirrel shifted the leaves of a tree or an acorn cracked against Dalia's tin roof. Once or twice she thought she heard tires again, and she stopped, looked up at nothing.

It was dark before they were finished with Bud, but there was light enough from the full moon and the stars to see. They were so far from city lights that they could even see the hazy river of the Milky Way splitting the sky. If they looked up, that is.

Dalia began stripping to her underwear, her dress ruined. "I got a call from his girl last week."

The world creaked and cranked as Mary rolled a metal barrel from under the shed, the bottom scraping as she tugged it off the uneven concrete that rimmed the building. She filled it with faded newspapers, dropped in her jeans, her T-shirt, Dalia's dress. "My bra clear?" she asked.

"Looks it."

"Soak the ground. There's been a lot of rain lately, but still a hot ash might catch this grass."

Dalia pulled the hose. "Daddy's matches are still in the shed," she said. "There's lighter fluid, too." Their father had often burned evidence here, gambling receipts, boxes from off the back of a truck, a dead drug dealer's clothes. "You not going to ask what she had to say?"

"Is it why you shot him?"

"Maybe. I don't know."

Mary added twigs and Spanish moss to the barrel, more newspaper, threw a match in. "You got to be kidding me, D. You don't know?" Her voice was loud, but there was no one around, no one to overhear.

Dalia ignored her. "She was crying."

"She claim he beat her?"

"Bud?" Dalia laughed. "No. No, of course not. She said he was leaving her. Begged me to give him back. Like he was mine, like I wanted him."

With everything damp, the fire was slow to catch, and Mary got the lighter fluid out, tried another match. "Did you?"

"No." The silence dragged on and Dalia watched the moss and wood and newspapers and bloody clothes light, watched the fire climb and fold itself over the edges of the barrel as if trapped and desperately needing escape. Watched it stay right where it was. "And, isn't that sad."

She had wanted Bud so badly when she was younger. Whenever she visited from LSU, he'd show up with magnolias that he'd pinched from the tree in the front yard, the one her daddy'd planted for her when she was six, her daddy saying they'd grow tall together. Bud always claimed that he'd bought the big white blooms, the both of them laughing as he pretended to search for a receipt.

The night her father had chased him off, she'd sounded just like the girl, Bud's stripper. "I love him," she'd screamed, her voice high pitched and panting, the sound of it climbing to fill every space in the kitchen.

Her father'd just stared at her. His eyes the sort of gray that blanketed the bayou in winter. She'd never yelled at him before, had never really cried, not since she was small. And there she was sobbing so hard that her body shook with it. It felt as if her teeth might rattle right out of her head.

Her daddy hadn't raised his voice, but it crackled like a bonfire. "You're hysterical and he's trash." He put his 12 gauge on the table. "And if he comes back, I'll shoot him. Now buck the hell up, sit the hell down, and calm yourself. You're scaring Mary." Her sister watching everything.

And she knew he would. Her daddy had no problem with killing.

After a while, Dalia looked away from the fire in the barrel and said, "I'm not sure when I stopped wanting Bud; I'm just sure I didn't want him anymore."

"Why don't you get dressed? I'll watch this" was her sister's only answer to that.

Along with a large cooler full of the meat, full of Bud, Dalia loaded a frog gig, a couple of Maglites, and some Cokes onto her boat—just in case they were stopped by the wildlife and fisheries boys—and waited for the sound of Mary's truck. She'd gone home for a shower, her badge, and her fishing license. "No need in taking any chances," she'd said.

The bayou was not a lonely or quiet place at night, and Dalia listened to the owls and crickets, watched the lightning bugs. She fought sleep, exhaustion creeping up on her as her boat rocked in the water. Once, she'd wanted to move to Baton Rouge or New Orleans, to be a doctor or an architect, but the cities hadn't suited her. She'd felt trapped by the concrete, the constant buzz of lights, the people pushing against each other. She missed home, never stayed gone long.

Now, she lived off of her father's pension and what Bud gave her, dreams of working, of being someone, lost to her wanderings in her daddy's garden. Mary always helped her out if things got tight.

Tonight there was a part of her that was afraid her sister wouldn't return, though, so when the grating rumble of tires on pea gravel interrupted the swamp song, it was a relief. She squinted at the lights and felt panicky when they stayed steady, even after the engine had cut. She imagined Mary staring at her, how she'd look in the harsh beams, and wondered if she hated her a little. As far as Dalia knew, Mary'd never taken a bribe or planted evidence, had never enjoyed the "tiny perks" their daddy'd so loved. She'd walked straight.

Eyes watering from the light, Dalia counted. One Mississippi. Two Mississippi. Three Mississippi. Her breath more shallow with each Mississippi. Finally, the lights winked out, and the sound of the door opening knocked her in the chest. Dalia could breathe again. But her eyes were light-blind so she couldn't see her sister's face. Mary said, "Last boat ride, D. I mean it," her voice hot and crackling like their daddy's.

And suddenly in her head, Dalia was screaming at her daddy all over again. That night in the kitchen. Screaming and begging incoherently. And she was grabbing his shotgun and running into the night.

"Last boat ride," she whispered as Mary got into Bud's boat, untied it. Then Dalia reached for the ropes that held hers, loosed it, and turned the motor over, following Mary down the river.

She imagined what it was like for Mary that night, watching from the doorway as their father chased her. Her sister had worshiped the man, following him around and playing sheriff with his badge, showing him their mud pies and laughing as he told fish stories. Cutting the vegetables as he cooked dinner. Pouring Beam for him to sip on the porch. Always a good daughter. Dalia knew that they'd hunted together long after she'd stopped going, and that after she left for college, they drank together, played cards together, even missed her together.

She barely knew her little sister when she came home for visits. Even though they were so close in age, she'd always thought of Mary as the baby, but the child had grown out of her quickly, the woman having moved in more and more each month.

Up ahead, Mary cut the motor, called out, "Here's good." So Dalia pulled alongside her and tried to hold the boats steady as her sister nimbly climbed from one to the other. "Let's go," she said, leaving Bud's boat to the current. Dalia handed her a Coke and turned the wheel.

They drove for a while and finally cut the engine to drift quietly into a set of smaller waterways that branched off from the main bayou. Cypress knees bumped the hull occasionally, and the water was shallow enough that a wrong turn could beach them. Maglites out, they scanned the marsh grasses with the beams, looking for the red glow of alligator eyes. Frog and spider eyes glow green or yellow under flashlight, and there were plenty of those, the frogs singing nonstop and sounding like ducks, their voices so big.

Finally they found a series of banks with red reflections and backed the boat a little ways away until they were upstream from what looked to be nesting grounds, the darkness thick with gator eyes.

"Here's good," Mary said. It was the first words they'd spoken in a while, and Dalia tried to read her sister's tone. She got nothing from it.

They worked quickly, dropping the meat in the water a bit at a time.

She remembered how surprised her father'd looked when she'd whirled on him, his own gun in her hands. His eyes were hidden in the darkness but his whole body'd shot straight up with the shock of it, and he'd lifted his palms a little. There was a small noise as if he was about to say "baby," as if the word was caught in his breath. Dalia still wasn't sure if she actually pulled the trigger that night or if the gun had just gone off. The feel of it kicking in her hands made her think it was alive, that maybe, maybe, it had propelled the shot on its own, maybe she'd done nothing but not stop it.

His face had opened like a flower, blooming horribly, and she'd stood there forever, expecting it to close again.

The sound of the meat hitting the water made her feel a little sick. "I did love him," she said to Mary, unsure of which man she meant.

It had been Mary who'd taken the gun from her that night, who had decided they should leave their father in the dark water. Mary who'd told the deputy that their father'd left to hunt and that they hadn't seen him since. Mary who'd mentioned a drug dealer from Dallas, mentioned that he'd been calling the house, leaving threats. Mary who'd run for sheriff so that Dalia would always be safe.

Dalia, on the other hand, had done nothing much except marry Bud.

Tossing the bits of the man she'd killed her daddy for into the black of the swamp, she thought of the morning her father floated back to them, of not understanding what the thing bumping the bank really was.

The fetid water churned and splashed as gar and bass and, finally, the alligators moved in, and the same sweet rot she'd smelled a million years ago, sitting on the bank with her daddy's body, filled her nose.

El Feo

Zee Toledo shifted in his waders, causing dark ripples to circle his legs like bullseyes. The body caught under the lip of his trap was a problem. He couldn't ignore it. It was a goddamn body. Looked like a man about his age, if the just-starting-to-gray mop of hair was any indication. It—he—was upside down, so Zee had little more to go on than the cloud of hair and a pair of brown trousers that looked a lot like his own. And the damn thing—the person—the body—was tangled in his property. For Zee, the problem was a practical one. He couldn't release and kill the large, squealing nutria inside the cage without first releasing the dead man.

But Zee was trespassing. Technically. And the trap was outside the Nutria Control Program Harvest Area. By a smidge. And every nutria Zee was carrying was worth a fiver in bounty and maybe more in fur and meat *if* he wasn't carrying it *here*. Just north of the boundary. Next to this floater.

Fifty bucks in tails already and he'd just started clearing the day's traps. There were ten left in this stretch of swamp, and Zee was bound and determined to get each and every bounty. His daughter's ninth was Saturday, and there was a fancy dollhouse out there with Isa's name on it.

Zee was not squeamish about touching the dead man. He spent his life covered in the gore of animals that others found too distasteful to hunt, eat, or keep. What he was concerned about was what touching a dead man might mean for him in the long run. So, Zee stood there, just looking between the trap and the body for a good five or ten minutes. Back and forth. A goddamn eternity for a man always in motion.

It wasn't an easy decision. Zee'd spent the first three years of his adulthood in Angola prison. He was sent there at seventeen and got out just before he turned twenty-one. A short-timer in Angola, where nearly everyone died in the jumpsuit, but a convict forever out here. He'd spent a lot of time since then promising himself, his wife, his kid, and his parole officer that he wasn't going back. And Zee'd kept that promise. And he meant to continue to keep it.

The body was face down and fat with bloat. He nudged it, and as if in protest, a hand the color of crab meat rose in the water. White man, then. Wedding ring. A nubbed thumb and forefinger that told Zee he was a worker. Blue collar corpse. It—he—Zee was having pronoun troubles. His wife Alina told him that what you called things and people and animals mattered. That the words you used all mattered. Zee tried to make himself think of this thing, this bag-of-dead as a person. So, "he." He smelled just like any other dead animal in the sun. Shitty, but not much different than the rest of the swamp.

Inside the wire trap was a fat, two-foot-long nutria, her front claws slipped between the mesh bottom so that they were deep in the shirt of the dead man under her, her back feet slipping for purchase on the branch-dam Zee'd set the cage against. He thought nutria looked more like beavers than rats. If you ignored the scaly snake of a tail, that is. And the foul, orange teeth. She was squealing and standing slumped. So her right back leg, looking limp and crumpled, was likely broken. Now that he was his own boss, not working under anyone else, and could decide how he spent his profits, he used only the humane traps. Still, the animals ended up in pain more often than he liked.

It was something he lied to Isa about. He promised her they never suffered. He thought of it as a Santa Claus lie, a small, good lie, and worked hard to make it as close to the truth as he could.

So even if he didn't need the bounty, he needed into that trap.

He owed her a clean death.

But the makeshift latch Zee used for the cage door was tangled up in the thick blue twine someone had wrapped around and around the corpse's neck, dark purple bruises peeking out from the twisted, crude noose. And the loose wires that Zee never bothered to clip from the trap's bottom gripped the man's shirt, which was twisted so far around by the nutria's scrambling that some of the front buttons were visible. The tight metal mesh of the trap was too small for him to deliver a blow through. His knife would not fit either. And Zee didn't own a gun. Never touched one. It wasn't worth the risk.

He checked for snakes before kneeling in the water to work at the body, trying not to worry about what he might leave on the dead man. What the cops might find there. What he didn't bother worrying about was knowing him, this man who was now a body. So when Zee finally did work the latch to the trap free, he didn't even pause to flip the man over and look at his face. He just finished the nutria, a quick, careful blow, cut her tail, and bagged her.

He was nearly back in the jon boat when he realized he'd have to take the trap. Couldn't leave it with the dead man. He'd have to gather all his other traps in the area, too. Just in case. That was when he turned the man over. Trying to work the rest of the trap free from the twisted shirt. That was when he saw the face. Bloated and greening at the edges. His P.O.

Zee'd finished his time on parole ten years ago, and when he did, he'd hugged Carl Landry, pounding him on the back. "*El Feo*," Zee said, by then comfortably using the name Landry's wife, a plump Puerto Rican who sort of reminded Zee of a younger version of one of his aunts, told him to call Landry the first time he visited their home. She'd piled Zee's plate high with smoked pork and jambalaya, then turned to pinch Carl's bony cheek, teasingly repeating, "El Feo." *The Ugly*.

It was different back then, Carl really too young to know better than to get close with his parolee, Zee too scared of going back to prison, too lonely on the outside, to not search for friendship in the only person he had to talk to. "I don't make a habit of inviting cons for dinner," Carl said gruffly, that first time, "But you look like you haven't had a meal in weeks, maybe more."

They ate together once every two or three months for the rest of Zee's long parole.

"Thank you. For everything, man," he said when it was finally done and they were hugging goodbye.

Carl patted his shoulder, then pushed him away as if to get a good look at his face. "Zacarias, just be good, dude. Be a man. Do your business. Take care of your girls. Stay out of bullshit."

That was what he'd told Zee the first time Zee met him, too: "Stay out of bullshit." Trying to seem tough then, not wanting Zee to know he was one of his very first parolees. He even let Zee think he'd lost the fingers in an altercation with another con. But he hadn't. Just a run of the mill factory accident before he got his degree.

It was Carl who'd told Zee about the nutria. Of course, back then the money was still great for fur and the bounty didn't yet exist. Carl who had a brother that trapped. Carl who hooked him up when Zee couldn't get hired anywhere he could stand working. Zee always fighting back then, throwing punches for the little guys that got screwed over at the sort of shitholes that were the only places willing to hire a spic con. Fighting himself right out of job after job. Carl clapping him on the back and calling him "Don Quixote" and keeping the ruckuses off the books.

By the time they were officially done with each other, they were very nearly friends. And almost certainly a strange sort of family.

Zee worked a pair of wire clippers between the cage and the body.

It was an impossible coincidence, Carl wedged here under his trap. But Zee couldn't figure how it would be anything but a coincidence. They didn't run in the same circles anymore. Zee stayed away from convicts—always, no matter what. Carl's life was built around them.

And though Zee's time in prison wasn't the only thing that connected the two men, it was most of it. They stayed in touch longer than was normal, Zee knew that. But still, it had faded to mostly Christmas cards.

The last real tie between them—Carl's brother Jack—died almost two years ago. Heart attack.

Zee snipped at the wires from the trap, trying not to cut the shirt, too. It was slow work. Snip, reposition, snip, reposition. He tried not to think about how long it was taking. How long he crouched there, water riding past his crotch as he shed skin cells and hair follicles over Carl's body.

Jack's wake was probably the last time Zee saw him. Saw him alive. Carl a little drunk and patting Isa on the head absently, marveling at what a weed she was. "God, you grow fast. She grew fast, huh?" Anything not to look at the closed casket or talk to the other mourners, it seemed. Carl alone at the funeral. Zee didn't have the heart to ask where his wife was, just in case.

The last of the hooked wires trimmed, Zee pulled at the trap and Carl's head jerked up, milky eyes pointed straight at him. "Jesus, Feo." He fingered the bit of twine between the trap and Carl's neck. "How the fuck did you get yourself into this." He didn't ask the corpse who put the cord there. It was an easy answer. A con.

"Spend your life with trouble, and it will finish you," Carl told him long ago. He meant Zee had to stay clear of his old friends from before prison. Had to lose himself now that he was out so that the men he'd aligned himself with at Angola couldn't saddle up to him on the outside. If they, too, somehow managed parole.

Carl didn't mean that being a P.O., that following trouble around for a living, would get *him*, would kill *him*, but Zee knew that it had.

Zee loaded the empty traps into the back of his truck, the nutria into coolers of dry ice. In his pocket were the bits of wire he'd pulled from Carl's shirt, and he played with them like he would a pocket full of coins, or when he was in prison and there were no coins, the pebbles he'd shuffle in his palm.

No one knew about the traps he laid in this part of the Atchafalaya. Not even his wife. Alina wouldn't have understood that the closest Harvest Area had its fair share of trappers already. That the nutria were as bad outside it as they were inside. That he was doing something good here. Something for Isa. Protecting her wetlands. Filling her plate.

That he needed this one small act of defiance.

So he'd kept it very secret. No one at all knew about the twenty traps out here.

He fished his cell from the ziplock he put the phone in when he was on the boat. "Isa, honey, get your mom, would you?" He jiggled the bits of metal in his pocket. "Tell her it's important. Emergency, *mija*."

He thought for a moment that he should lie to Alina. Just tell her he was running late, but she'd told him on their wedding day, "No lies, no lies ever." And he'd nodded and told her nearly everything since.

"El Feo's dead," he said when she got on the line. Then he told her about finding the body under the squealing nutria, about his special spot. About keeping it from her. The lie of omission. All in one breath, gripped by a sudden fear that this coincidence was much more dangerous than he'd been able to imagine out in the swamp.

"Carl's dead?"

"I don't know what to do. Alina, I left him out there, where I found him, left him bloating in the sun. I left him to—" Zee shook his head as if she could see him. "Something is going to eat him. I left him to that."

"Who knows you trap there?"

"No. No one knows. No one."

"Someone. Someone knows. Someone put Carl there, Zee." She said something to Isa, a mumble and Zee imagined her with the phone to her chest, the way she did when she talked to her mother, whispering her frustrations to him while his mother-in-law ranted into her T-shirt. When she came back, her voice was low and he realized she'd sent Isa out of the room. "Someone fucking murdered Carl and planted him on you. On us. Someone goddamn knows. Think, Zee."

But he couldn't think of anyone. He'd first gone out to the little sheltered cove of wetland when he started working for Carl's brother.

Jack was friends with the owner, an old woman who had no interest in fishing or trapping, and didn't have any other family that wanted to work the land. But the area was hard to reach and Jack had given up on the sheltered bit of swamp as he aged. Zee didn't trap there again until after Jack's heart attack. And he'd never even seen anyone else fish there. Not another boat in the months he'd been going to the spot. "Do you really think—"

"Don't you?"

"There is a bit of cash in my desk." He liked to buy Isa a present just from him every year. Something he picked out without Alina. She was so practical and always knew just what their daughter wanted and needed. But he liked to go off script, and Alina liked to see him grin over his secret gifts. They were good together. "There's a dollhouse in town."

"Jesus, Zee."

"Maybe I can figure this out quick. But I can't bring this, whatever the hell this is, to our door, baby. To you and Isa." One of the pieces of metal in his hand was more jagged than the others and he rubbed his finger over the sharp of its end over and over, concentrating on the bit of pain there. "Just in case, go to the antique store on 1st. The weird little building, you know? With the mural?" Alina made a small noise. "They have—you wouldn't believe it. You know that house Isa built in her game, what is it?"

"Minecraft."

"Yeah, you know that house she built? That mansion? They have a dollhouse that looks just like it. It's amazing, baby. Little triangle roofs, bits of decorative timber? Like something in a movie about rich people up north."

"Tudor," Alina said, her voice too quiet. She'd helped Isa with her little project in the game, the two of them bent over architecture books they'd taken from the library. His girls so much smarter than Zee.

"I don't think there's enough money in the drawer, but maybe you could talk to the woman—"

"I'll take care of it," she said.

Zee wanted to tell her everything was going to be okay, but she would just tell him not to lie, her voice bent around fear and sadness, building a little safe space for her heart to hide in, a little cell away from him and this violence and whatever the future now held. He couldn't stand the thought of it, so Zee just kept talking about the dollhouse instead.

Carl lived on one of those streets with no trees. The houses all looked the same, small, brick places with fancy doors and no yards, a dented pickup or cheap coup sitting in each drive in the evenings. During the day, they were mostly empty, but last Zee knew, Carl's wife Sophia worked from home, clicking away on the computer in a nook in the kitchen.

He didn't know what he'd say to her, but he couldn't figure where else to go. He circled the block two, three, four times, trying to write a script for himself. He couldn't tell her he found Carl. Couldn't even say the man was dead, could he? Zee pulled into the empty drive of a home with a "For Sale" sign and an overgrown yard. Stared at Carl's house as if willing the man to appear, to not be rotting in the swamp. Instead, it was Sophia who stepped outside, her arms around her torso as if she was somehow cold in the middle of August. She looked down the street in both directions. Then tilted her head as if she'd caught sight of his filthy truck with its red mismatched bumper, easy to recognize.

Uncertain whether to get out and greet her or to start the engine and just drive away, he sat there until it was too late and she was at the window.

"Zee?"

He rolled it down and looked at her without opening the door. She'd lost some weight and it hardened her face. The plump of her cheeks had once kept her young, while Zee and Carl wore each year, piling them on, but now she'd caught up with them. With him.

"Carl didn't send you?" She peered into his truck as if to find her husband hiding behind him in the small cab. "Are you spying?"

"No, I—" Zee opened the door. "Can we talk?"

Sophia looked behind her, searching the street again. "I have a friend coming."

Words fell from his mouth, a jumble, a rush, "I found Carl," and her head shot up, and Zee caught himself. "I found Carl's, one of Carl's sets of reading glasses the other day, made me want to come say hi."

"Parked at the neighbor's?"

He didn't answer.

"Whatever. He ain't here anymore. He's down in Baton Rouge," she paused and turned at the sound of a car, body tense, "Or somewhere. I don't know where he is. Why would I?"

Zee wasn't sure what to say to that, and he fidgeted in the silence until the sound of another vehicle filled it. A work truck this time. They both watched it pull into her driveway, trimmers and a mower bounced in the bed as it squeaked to a stop. Gardener. Shitty driver.

She didn't turn back to Zee. "It's been over between us. Long time. So if he owes you money, I can't help you. Mira, I got to go."

Sophia moved quickly down the sidewalk to her house, not once looking back at him. She didn't stop as she passed the truck in her drive but she did tuck her head down and turn it towards whoever was inside, saying something before shuffling into her home. After a few beats, a guy got out and lit a cigarette. Zee didn't recognize him, exactly. But the ink on his arms, scratchy, blue-black, and faded, he was pretty sure that was prison ink. Zee rubbed his hand, the three blue dots near his thumb were the same washed out color. They never let him forget who he had been. Who he was.

Zee found a booth he could see the road from and sat down with his coffee. He didn't normally come to McDonald's, but Zee figured chances were better than not that the gardener would have to pass by here when he left. There weren't a lot of roads out of Carl's shitty neighborhood. Zee didn't know what he'd do when—if—the truck passed, maybe try Sophia again, maybe not.

Carl had a rule. He didn't hire cons himself. If he liked you, really, really liked you and believed in you, he'd find you something, maybe even with family like he did for Zee. But he wouldn't hire you himself. It'd be a breach. Of course, a lot of cons did lawn work. It was outside and you worked it alone. And there were no background checks. And everyone knew it was a good way to case the next job that'd either make you rich or get you thrown right back in the pen.

So, it wasn't that odd. The gardener and his tattoos. Not really.

But Sophia had said she was waiting for a friend.

And the gardener had gone inside.

Zee knew Carl and Sophia's marriage had been rocky. He was bad with money, lending it to good-for-nothings with sob stories like Zee, and it pissed her off. And she had a wandering eye. It had wandered Zee's way once. Before Alina. Just the one time. Jacking him off in the kitchen after Carl ran out to take care of another good-for-nothing's crisis. Carl a good guy like that. And Zee, back against the blue pantry door, unsure of how to escape the situation and then, her hand tight around him, not wanting to.

So maybe Sophia had a type.

But if Carl'd moved out, she could fuck who ever she wanted. And it certainly had nothing to do with Zee. Nothing to do with his traps or his life. His freedom. Sophia had no beef with him that he knew. He watched the road and searched his brain, but he didn't know the gardener. He was sure of it. So no beef there either.

If they had killed Carl, they had no reason to involve him.

Finally the truck passed. And Zee half stood in the booth, an involuntary action that gave him a better view. He wondered if the guy used thick, blue twine to tie roses to stakes. Or if those tools were strapped to the bed of his truck with the cording. If maybe there was some in Sophia's craft supplies. It seemed laughable, imagining this woman he knew, who he'd known for over a decade, who may have been flawed, but was also kind and welcoming and sweet and funny, imagining her a mastermind in Carl's murder. Laughable. And still Zee kept his eyes on the truck. It swung widely onto the ramp to the interstate, the setting summer sun lighting ablaze the chrome accents along the bed and tires and doors.

This time Zee parked in Carl's driveway, but once again he paused before getting out. He reached for his cell in the glove box. Maybe Isa was done with soccer practice.

"She's on the field now. I could wave her over?" He could hear the wind whipping around Alina's face. It was his afternoon to drive Isa. To watch her bounce across the muddy field.

"No, it's okay. I'll call after I try Sophia again. Any noise over there?"

"*Nada*. No cops, at least. Nothing on the TV."

"Was there enough for the dollhouse? What'd you call it? The Tudor?"

Alina didn't answer right away. "Maybe we can borrow some from the piggy bank. Pay her back with interest before she even knows it's gone." They'd done it occasionally for gas money and last year when they'd run short around Easter, replacing her birthday and tooth fairy dollars with fives and tens out of guilt. It was no big deal, Zee knew, but suddenly there was a rage in him that neither Carl's dead body or the realization that someone had framed him for the murder had instilled in Zee.

"Just be careful," Alina said. "Don't confront anyone."

And Zee, not wanting to lie, said he loved her, instead of, "I won't."

Sophia came to the door with a kid, maybe one or so, on her hip. Her eyes were puffy, her face and neck splotchy. "What do you want, Zee?" She sounded tired.

"Can we talk?" He didn't try to hide his anger.

She opened the door wide and moved into the kitchen, leaving Zee to close it and follow her or not, the child bouncing on her new, narrower hips.

"Who's this?"

"My kid. And don't fucking take that tone in my house. Feo's kid. That was your next question? If she's his?"

"I didn't have a next—"

"Why are you here, Zee?"

He slipped into one of the little chairs at their kitchenette, the same table and chairs he'd sat in the first time over, now scratched and wobbly and missing their cushions. "What's going on here? With you? With Carl?"

Sophia moved around and around the kitchen, her steps jagged and frantic, the baby threatening to cry whenever she stopped. "You know he was the handsomest man I'd ever seen when we met. So handsome, I was, you know, breathless. *Flechazo.* Struck. So I called him El Feo, you know to tease him a little, give me some courage to talk to him, and he was so cocky, he laughed. Fucker." She paused for a moment, catching her breath a bit, and the kid screwed up her face, started turning red. Sophia sighed and went back to pacing again. "But you know, that was a million years ago. Today, I just got this. You want to talk to Carl, he ain't here."

Zee reached for the kid. "Let me try. Isa was fussy, too."

"He owe you money? That what this is about? Because it's tight here already. I can't help you, Zee. I know how it must be for you and Alina, with her out of work and all, but I don't got nothing I can spare." Sophia slumped into one of the chairs. Put her head in her hands.

"No. Of course not." The kid stiffened her chubby arms and legs, fighting him, but Zee put his head to hers and murmured into her black hair, rocking a little until she relaxed into the plane of his chest. "Why would he?"

The look on Sophia's face said she thought he was stupid.

"Who did he owe money, Sophia?"

"Everyone but you, I guess." She watched him weave around the small kitchen with her daughter. "If it isn't dogs, it's cocks. Whatever bets he can find, right?" When Zee didn't answer, she laughed. "You didn't know? Seriously? Why do you think he buddied up to you, *chico*? When my good-for-nothing cousin got sent up for fighting birds, Feo pounced on the first con he saw with brownish skin and a Latin name. Don't tell me he chickened out and never asked you."

He had, though. After the first dinner, while they smoked cigarettes on the back porch. Zee thought Carl was joking and had laughed. "Sure. Cocks. My daddy fights them. My uncle sacrifices them. And my *tia* sucks 'em." Carl'd laughed and pounded him on the back so hard he'd lost his smoke in the grass and had to stamp it out. He loved to tell the story over a beer, and until today Zee'd always thought it was just a joke.

"All these years, and you working for Jack and everything. You seriously didn't know?" She shook her head. "After they got Jack, I told Carl, it was me or the gambling." She watched Zee rock and bounce the baby. "And I was always stupid enough to believe him when he chose me. But, I'm done, Zee. I don't even got a number to give you. Call the office. He transferred, but they can tell you, I'm sure."

"What do you mean they got, Jack? It was his heart. You don't give someone a shitty heart."

"You do if you threaten to take a finger for every grand they owe you, while you beat the interest out of them. Especially if they owe you more money than they got fingers."

The baby in his arms let out a soft snort. A little congested baby snore. The noise Isa made when she was on the front end of a cold. Even now as old as she was, there was this little snort as she drifted off on the couch that told him and Alina to buy lots of orange juice.

"They called my house. Can you believe that shit? Not even El Feo's cell. They called my damn house to tell him he could pick up his brother in the goddamn swamp. And he was at the fights again in less than a month. Then six months clean, before he went out to lose the mortgage check. Then clean. Then calls to his cell again. Leaving at night. Lies. Borrowing money again. So fuck him." She stood up, pulled the baby from Zee's arms. "But if I were you, I'd stay clear. El Feo isn't worth your visit."

"He's dead, Sophia. I found his body tangled in one of my traps this morning."

She didn't say anything. She didn't cry out. Didn't sob. "I got a payment plan worked out. Thousand-dollar lawn cuts until they say I'm done."

Zee kept his voice as low as he could. "You fucking knew? Why? Why me? My traps?"

She laid the baby in a small playpen in the living area before answering. "I don't know where you were laying those things, Zee. But I wouldn't go back there. Or come back here."

Zee pulled into the nutria collection center, but there were no other trucks in the lot, no lights on. He'd get no bounties today and would have to freeze his tails. He put his head on the steering wheel. Unsure of what to do now.

He needed to call his girls. But instead he just sat there, eyes closed, forehead sweating against the black vinyl.

The first time Jack took Zee through the tight clutch of tupelo-gum trees and tangled reeds that guarded his special spot, he'd said, "Think skinny," seconds before the boat got stuck. He knew it was coming. The only reason Zee, young and impatient and afraid of alligators and gar, hadn't quit instead of jumping into the fetid water and pulling the boat past the mess of plants was Carl.

Carl who'd made him promise to try, saying, "My brother's like you, hot headed, not suited for a lot of jobs. This works for him. And you know, if you can't find something, some job *you* can make work, they'll put you back inside."

Carl who'd kept him out of the pen.

So he'd jumped in, even though he couldn't see the swamp bottom, the water so dark, and he pulled hard. Jack letting him do the bull's work of the job and saying, "It's worth it. No one comes back here. No other trappers. It's private land."

"You own all this?" Zee was impressed.

"Me? No, I got a pot to piss in and a bed and that's about all I need. This is a benefactor's land."

Now, after everything Sophia'd said, it sounded evasive. The way Jack had talked. But at the time, Zee barely knew that word. Benefactor. He hadn't gone to school much. Not like Alina.

She was still so out of his league. But back then, if he hadn't stayed working for Jack, if it hadn't been for Carl, he never would have asked her out. Whatever was lower than not-good-enough, that's what he'd been.

Sitting in his truck, head against the wheel, he realized Jack had never told him whose land it was. Carl had been the one. Carl told him about the old lady when Zee'd gone in for his next pee test. "She, you know, farms. Raises chickens and shit."

Zee hadn't even wondered at that. Farming animals out there. He just believed. He'd heard of swamp cows. Why not chickens? Besides, Carl was a guy Zee somehow always just believed.

And it had worked out well for him.

He'd heard the cocks, over there, though. Crowing at each other. A hell of a noise that carried. No buildings or roads or people out that way to buffer it. So it filled the swamp, startling him every time one would scream. But Jack had never been bothered by it. "Used to it," he said. And Zee just thought how lonely it made it feel out there, that big noise from such a small animal, like if he got lost no one would ever find him at all.

A perfect place to dump a body, whether Zee had ever gone back out that way or not.

Whether it was his traps or someone else's or no traps at all.

Zee started the truck and called his wife. Told her he was coming home.

That night, on the couch, their daughter curled tightly between them and snoring a bit, that soft snort telling them she'd have a cold for her birthday party, Zee asked Alina if they could send Sophia some money. He had no living parents. No church. No religion. He had Alina. He had Isa. He'd had Carl. Whoever Carl was. The money would be a tithe to the only thing he believed in. Alms to the man who'd given him what little he had. And a gamble. A bet on the corpse never, ever being found or attached to Zee and his traps. "I know it's not my debt," he said. "And we don't really have much extra."

Alina laid her hand on his, so they both were touching their daughter's head on his lap, and nodded. Carl'd visited the hospital when Isa was born. "¡Mira, Feo! Look at what we made," Zee'd said. And Carl clapped him on the back and took some of the credit. "We sure as hell did."

Zee sat as still as he could, his hand under Alina's, their daughter between them, and watched her sleep, the faded, scratchy, blue-black tattoo on his hand moving with each of her small breaths.

Everything Shining

Teenie leaned against the back door, shoulder to glass, and considered the fat, black water moccasin lazing on the slab outside. He didn't see the orange tom that'd been coming around lately, the too-lean cat with only one eye and a ragged bit missing from both ears. Most evenings, it would sweetly pluck scraps of steak and catfish from his fingers, and Teenie'd gotten used to him. He figured the tom was probably somewhere cooler than his usual spot on the stained slab, snoozing under one of the camellias or his momma's roses, thank god, what with the moccasin fatter around than probably all four of the tom's thin legs put together—the snake a winner in that fight, for sure.

Teenie considered the shotgun in the closet, but grabbed a sharp-edged shovel out of the garage instead. He hated to kill the snake, but he knew the tom wouldn't survive a bite. Hell, he might not survive one either, not with the Ford blowing black smoke and his cell service turned off. Teenie sighed, stepped out the back door, and swung the shovel twice, hard.

The clang of metal to concrete still ringing in his ears, Teenie lifted the snake's head with the shovel, squinting as he carried it back to the coulee, filled with water after the recent rains. The summer sun seemed extra bright these days—the light kicking off the pile of copper his cousin Ray'd dumped in the back. The UV index was off the charts, the weather channel said. Wear sun block, it advised. Teenie didn't have any, but Ida,

Ray's wife, was forever talking about how they were all going to burn up, Teenie never quite sure if she meant that hell or UV would be the cause.

Teenie took his time moving across his half acre. He was a long legged man who strolled with a lazy, rolling limp ever since he took a tumble on a rig, but still sweat pricked at his shaved scalp and stung his cracked lips, and he figured he might should buy some sun block, just in case.

He didn't like how Ray's scrap metal pile was growing, the copper wire a twisted mess in his yard, like a strange nest or even a mass of shining, curling snakes. About ten hastily cut pipes and a parking meter pregnant with quarters topped off Ray's ever-expanding haul.

"I'm not your fucking bank, Ray," he'd said, last time that his cousin dropped some off.

"You're not much fucking else, Teenie," Ray had said back, tossing a Miller at him. Ray's wife just shrugged her skinny shoulders when Teenie looked to her for help. He wondered sometimes if Ray didn't feed Ida, keeping her hungry like a fighting dog or something.

As he took the snake's body to join its head at the coulee, Teenie watched the sun play against the scales, the black not absorbing the light like you'd think, but slinging it out like polished metal. Everything in his yard shining like that these days.

"All this glittering, you'd think we were rich," he said to no one at all as he watched the snake float away.

Later he told the tom about it. "You be careful, don't get bit by one of those black bastards," he said, offering the back of his hand for the cat to butt up against. A car's engine caught his attention, and he scratched at the base of one of the cat's ruined ears. "And stay clear of Ray's truck when he pulls up. The sumbitch drives too fast, won't even see you."

Pretty much no one but Ray and Ida drove down Teenie's road. It was a potholed dead-end the parish had let his daddy name a million years ago: Whiskey Lane, as if he was a bootlegger instead of just a crippled dreamer with a half-built radiator still. Teenie's momma had huffed every time she pulled past the sign, sick of her husband's schemes. The both of them dead now, but Teenie imagined them still bickering over that sign every time he hit the end of his road.

Ray thought the name was hilarious, still chuckling over it, Teenie's daddy some kind of comic god to him.

The sound of the engine drew closer, and Teenie went inside and pulled out some sandwich stuff. The front door slammed open and Teenie cursed.

"Hey, cuz?" Ray called into the house.

Teenie didn't bother playing out the fight he saw coming, instead saying, "Last time. I mean it," to his cousin, then, after a pause, "and don't hit my goddamn cat when you're pulling around."

The door popped closed in answer.

Ida wandered into the kitchen, all swoosh, swoosh in her short denim skirt, like she was still in high school. "You got a cat?" she asked, her voice somehow husky and girlish all at once.

Teenie shrugged, handed her a sandwich, watching her carefully to see if she'd take a bite. Her pale legs were just knees and angles, spotted by a bruise or two. She spent her evenings helping Ray get the copper wire out of new construction and was always covered in the marks of their "business." Ray said she could climb as good as a monkey, scrambling over just about anything. His helpful girl.

"Lucky. Ray won't let me keep anything alive around." She looked at the sandwich, one of her limp, brown curls sliding into the mustard as she lowered her head to inspect it. "I don't eat meat. It's bad for your colon."

Teenie nodded. Ida was constantly going on about colons. "Don't think there's much meat in that bologna. I can make you one with just cheese, I guess."

Ida shrugged and took a bite of the one he'd already made, mustard still in her hair. "It's bad for the environment too, meat eating. And ungodly. I read that..."

Teenie stopped listening, continued nodding as he washed the mayonnaise off the knife, put away the bread, the bologna. He liked the sound of her voice filling the nooks of his kitchen, but figured most of what she said was as good as white noise.

"You and Ray gonna have to sell that stuff soon," he said when there was a lull.

"That's all him." She grinned, and Teenie searched for anger or sarcasm or irony in her voice when she added, "He says that I'm too pretty to worry about it, anyway." He didn't find any.

Teenie nodded, and the back door opened. Ray was younger by two years, but he out bulked and out stood Teenie by a good fifty pounds and four inches. "Don't be so impatient, cuz," Ray said, using his dirty T-shirt to wipe sweat from his face. "You're going to get a nice chunk of rent money for the lawn space soon enough."

"I'd rather have my yard back."

"The shit you would. That truck of yours needs new rings," Ray poked him, square in the middle of his work shirt, finger thudding. "And it ain't like you're getting any calls to go out these days." Then came the crooked smile, all lip, his teeth covered like Ray'd never bothered to do when they were kids. Back then that smile was what he called gold for pussy. "You need me and my rent, cuz, and I need you." Ray didn't stop poking.

Teenie pulled away from the finger, thinking of how he'd got canned after slipping on the rig. Not following procedure, they'd said, making the fall his fault. An OSHA violation was the last thing he needed following him around. The rigs might not seem to take safety seriously, but they certainly took the possibility of being noticed by OSHA and MMS serious enough, especially since the big spill. And now no one in oil would hire him. He was blacklisted, not even the shallow water death traps called him back, lax as they were. And his back was as bad off as his truck these days, so what could he do? But then, maybe he wasn't too bad off to take a swing at Ray if the sumbitch kept poking.

Then Ray was saying, "Aww, come on. Look, I brought you a gift. Good shit," sweeping his arm out at Ida, all grand like. "Rack em, girl."

She pulled a fifth of drugstore tequila from her bag and lined up some paper cups from the cabinet. Ray stood there, arm still out, grinning like an asshole, like he fucking invented tequila, like he expected Teenie to start clapping.

They tossed back the shots, and Ray told Teenie all about a nearby substation he was pretty sure wasn't guarded too good. Teenie told him not to shit where they all ate. He had enough fucking copper he didn't know how to sell. They put back another round, and then another, and Ida said, "Teenie says I can name his cat," and Teenie nodded as if he'd told this girl he'd loved way back in high school any such thing.

The sound of someone banging around in his bathroom woke Teenie, and from his place on the carpet he could see that Ray was still passed out on the couch. There was a clanging crash, a bright noise he worried was the back of the toilet tank slipping, cracking as Ida searched for his back pills. He'd just started hiding them, tired of there never being one when he needed it. But he had no interest now in listening to Ida search and no will to confront her. So he pushed himself up, found the bag of cat food, what was left of last night's tequila, and his book, and turned the knob of the back door with his elbow, wishing she'd at least be quiet about it, that she'd sneak around, pretend that she didn't know that he knew she was stealing from him.

Teenie stepped into the night air, wet and heavy and hard to breathe. Bull frogs sounding like ducks, their voices so big out here, called to each other. The moon seemed barely a sliver, the rest of its fullness behind clouds, but the soft, blue haze of city lights that never left the horizon anymore made it easy enough for Teenie to see. After spilling some food on the concrete for the tom, he settled into the cypress rocker his mother made when he was about sixteen. "No use letting the tools rust," she'd said out in the shop, showing him how to sand the grey wood, how to measure the curve of the runners so they'd fall smooth and flat. That day, thanks to his mother, his father's plan to sell driftwood he'd stolen off of state land—any of his father's great plans, really—finally resulted in something Teenie could actually see, something he could touch.

All the while they were out there sweating over the cypress, Ray and his dad sat inside smoking and laughing. Dreaming bigger, they called it.

Setting the tequila bottle between his thighs and the book on his lap, Teenie thought about his dream—not so big, maybe. He'd figured on working offshore for a few years, ten or so, and putting enough money away to start a real business. Not some back of the yard, piece of shit scam, but a hardware store or a gas station. Maybe a little bar. He clicked his tongue, a quiet call, and the tom was there, ignoring the food to push at his hand, rubbing the sides of his teeth across Teenie's knuckles, his purring a heavy vibration against Teenie's skin. There were no savings though. The first little bit went to bury his mother in the family plot, and what he'd saved all these years since was now gone too, swallowed up by hospital bills and the time out of work.

The door made a noise and Ida was standing there with them, grinning wide, her teeth black in the shadows. "You can't read in the dark," she said, and Teenie thought she might be shaking a bit, then thought maybe it was just the tremor of his own hangover.

"Got a flashlight," he said, gesturing under the chair, and she was reaching between his thighs for the bottle, yanking on it in a way that told Teenie his pills were still under his mattress. The cat wandered to the spilled food.

"You always were a book guy," she said, settling to the concrete, her lips staying close to the mouth of the bottle. "Even in high school."

Teenie watched the tom and thought of Ida back then, always smoking by the dumpster, Ray's hand at the small of her back, his fingers down in the gap her jeans made there. Thought of the three of them riding around in Ray's truck, never anywhere to go but the levee, their stolen beers and pot making it almost interesting out there. Her face was rounder then, the skin pink at the edges instead of the hollow yellow-gray it had become. Wherever they went, Teenie ended up in a book, mostly so he didn't have to watch her make out with Ray. Then later, when Ray passed out, he'd put the book down and watch her fiddle with her cigarettes or the pulled wrapper from a beer bottle, the two of them sometimes talking about their lives in that golden time after Ray was out.

"We could name him after that guy in that book they made us read," she said, and Teenie almost said "Who?" but then caught up with her. The tom.

"Name him what you like," he said, still unsure of the book.

"Higgen?" She ran her hand across his leg. "Holden?" and Teenie thought of how he'd hated *The Catcher in the Rye*, how he'd hated selfish, snide Holden Caulfield, how everyone else had loved him.

"Sure," he said, brushing her bony fingers from his thigh and then imagining them still there. Knowing he was betraying the tom, he said, "Holden's good."

The next night when the lights popped, there was no lightning in the sky, no rain or heavy winds, no reason but his own empty bank account to be sweating in the dark. Teenie cursed himself for forgetting to pay the bill. He slipped outside and tried to do the math in his head, pacing the backyard with Holden following him, the both of them stopping and staring at Ray's pile of copper, that sort of "one day" treasure no good for paying a reconnect fee.

He could hear Holden purring, could hear the bull frogs extra loud, and then he realized he didn't hear anything else, not even the one buzzing street light. Everything was dark. He moved to the side of the lot, trying to remember if he could usually see the house down the way, trying to remember if he could always hear the crickets so loud.

Then there was the angry sound of a gunned engine and of tires spitting gravel and Holden was high tailing it to the back. Teenie turned and watched the cat even as he heard Ray's truck hit the driveway. He could hear a pounding from the front door and finally he looked back and Ray was standing there, just another shadow in the dark. But the pounding was too hard and the shadow was too erect, weirdly stiff and lacking Ray's easy slump. And it was alone.

Ray was alone.

Ida was not there. The taste of metal suddenly filled the back of Teenie's throat. The date flicked into his head, and he realized it was too early in the month for a disconnect.

Ida always following Ray. For fifteen years, Ida always in his footsteps. Always.

Ida just not there now.

And then Teenie knew why the lights were out. Copper.

His feet shifted in the slick mud as if waiting for a command, and then he was running, his boots fighting for traction. When he got to the front, he shoved Ray hard. "Where is she? Where the fuck, Ray?"

And Ray was shaking his head. "She wasn't even touching anything."

"You didn't leave her? Jesus."

Ray still shaking his head, "I put her out. There was a flash. She wasn't even touching anything and then this flash and," Ray finally stopped shaking his head and looked at his cousin. "Jesus, Teenie, she was on fire."

Teenie stared at Ray. "You didn't leave her there." His voice was matter of fact, and he went over to the truck, looked in the cab, in the bed, screaming at Ray now, "You didn't fucking leave her." And then he was back at the front door where Ray was standing and then inside and then getting his Daddy's wheelchair out of the spare room and then back at the truck putting the wheelchair in the bed. "Get the fuck in the truck, Ray," he said.

And Ray just staring at him, mouth open so even in the dark Teenie could see his ruined teeth, the bulk of them eaten away, leaving them sharp and crooked like fangs. "You fucking shortcut-taking junkie. Get in the truck or I'm getting the shotgun and shooting your ass where you stand." Teenie felt himself panting.

"It's not my—" and Teenie knew Ray was about to say "fault."

"Electricity jumps when it's hot, Ray. Arcing. It's fucking called arcing and, for what? Just to steal a thousand dollars' worth of scrap metal you can't even sell? For that, you took her someplace really hot?" Teenie looked at his dark house, the dark street lamp. "Really fucking hot?"

Ray started shaking his head again, but he moved finally, and Teenie could hear the soles of Ray's shoes scraping the driveway as he slinked over to the truck. The sound of it way too loud.

The substation was small, surprisingly small, as if it would hold only a little electricity. It was barely a shotgun patch of land where not much at all could have ever lived, where not even a bootlegger would bother to squat. As they pulled up, something seemed familiar. The smell. It reminded Teenie of a cochon de lait, and even as he thought of those roasts his father would throw when a scheme went well, he realized what he smelled now was no pig. A cloud moved a fraction and the light from the full summer moon, huge and orange, suddenly hit the edge of her hand, glittering against the sheen of her blackened fingernail. Teenie threw up in the truck.

So, at least his stomach was empty when he saw the rest of Ida.

Getting at her was not easy, even after they'd cut out a chunk of the fence, and Teenie could hardly bear any of it, not the walking to her, not the picking her up, not the carrying her like she was just one of his father's pigs. There was a quarter-sized patch on her forehead that somehow was still her sweet pale skin in a sea of thin black meat. Teenie set his eyes on a freckle there in the middle of it, one she'd had as long as he'd known her, and kept the mantra of her name rolling over and over his tongue as they walked.

Neither man knew how or where to hold this cracked and blacked version of Ray's helpful girl, so Teenie just tried to be gentle, but the skin of her left arm, crackling like tin foil, tried to slough as they moved her, and she was still so very hot to the touch even through the blanket Ray'd thrown on her to put out the fire. The blanket he'd left when he'd left her. Even with that shroud protecting their hands, the heat bit at them.

Her face was bloated and broken, the skin around her left eye especially swollen, creating a crack that threatened to split near the orb. He wondered if that was where the current had entered or exited, unsure of where the damage would be the worst, but he could still see her in there, in that freckle, that small patch of clear skin, and he would not look away.

They moved her to the wheelchair, her body small enough so that Teenie's back barely complained. Then he realized they'd have to take her out again to get her in the truck, the bed the only place that made sense, but he still thought maybe she could sit in the cab. Wanted to put her there, sitting up like she was still alive.

All the while he tried to imagine this was some other thing they were holding, some other thing they were out to do. But he couldn't. It was Ida.

"Hurry," Ray said, and Teenie tried to not hear him. "With lights out everywhere, someone will be out here soon to check," Ray now composed, Teenie the one just shaking his head.

The drive back was short, Teenie thinking of the huge pile of stolen copper at the back of his yard instead of the dead woman in the bed of Ray's truck.

Their grandfather had owned acres and acres of sugarcane fields once, but Teenie's father hadn't been interested in farming and then, after the wheelchair, wasn't able to do the work, even if he'd been willing. So he'd sold the fields off a parcel at a time, the money for each piece of family land never enough to do more than buy whiskey and dreams and disappointment. But there was one parcel no one ever bought, the little family cemetery started for Teenie's four stillborn aunts and uncles and later filled up with his grandparents, then Ray's daddy (shot while his son was still in the crib), a drowned cousin, and finally Teenie's parents. All of them in tombs like small stone beds, hard and flat and gray, everyone above ground here.

"She should be with the family," Teenie'd said in the truck.

And so the two men ended up behind someone else's fields, straining to pry open Teenie's mother's little tomb with a couple of crowbars from the big metal tool box next to Ida's head. Her grave was small, but it was the biggest one in the plot, Teenie spending all that he could when she died. The smell of dusty rot filled the air when the top slid sideways, and they pushed until the space was big enough. Grunting, they lowered Ida's curled body, wrapped in her rough shroud, into the stone bed, laying it so it was bowed around his mother's corpse. Teenie imagined the painted stone cherubs on the babies' graves watching them with their chipped blue eyes.

Then Ray moved to the truck too quickly, uttering no words over his wife's grave even, and Teenie watched him and, for just a minute, imagined splitting Ray's skull. Then, thinking of his momma shifting his cousin, just a squalling baby then, into his lap at Ray's father's funeral, thinking of her voice stiff and quiet as she explained that him and Ray'd be like brothers now, Teenie felt guilty.

"The police are bound to end up at your place soon enough," he said to Ray, and then under his breath to Ida and his mother, "and then mine."

Ray nodded, his hand on the door handle, and Teenie understood that Ray would slither away, leaving him with all that tangled, shiny evidence in his yard, too broke to pay the bail he was sure to need soon enough. He looked down at the flat grey tomb, closed again, and thought of his mother at the end, scrubbing other people's floors despite the cancer, his father's debts their only inheritance.

Ray and his father, the same man, really.

"A drink, maybe," Teenie said, knowing Ray would not turn him down.

When he went to pour the vodka, Teenie left his pills on the table, saying, "It's been a long night," as if he'd understand if Ray needed one or two, as if he was happy to share, and when he handed Ray a cup, he noticed the bottle'd moved, skidded to the left like it too was ready to run.

Teenie'd thought Ray would pass out fast, that maybe he'd call the cops once his cousin was snoring, but Ray was jumpy, talking a thousand words a minute, saying, "Maybe California. Maybe Vermont," going on about pot farming, already on to the next scheme. Ida's name never even coming up.

"What about the mess back there?" Teenie finally said, knocking on the glass of the back door in case Ray wasn't sure where he meant. Without any light shining on it, the treasure was just a grey lump.

Ray shrugged. "Don't think I got the time to find a buyer," he said, "I'll have to do without that cash."

Teenie looked at his reflection in the glass, saw his father's face outlined by the pile in the backyard. He jerked his head away and looked over at Ray. "You'll have to.... What the fuck is wrong with you?"

And Ray was saying, "Aw, come on, cuz. Be cool."

The shovel was still propped against the back door where he'd left it the morning before. "She loved you," Teenie said, his hand finding the handle, just meaning to lean on it like a cane, his back hurting so bad now.

Then Ray shrugged again, and Teenie sort of limped towards him, the head of the shovel a dull thump on the bare floor.

"You can't leave me with this mess," he said, and Ray turned and smiled at him, raised the paper cup in some sort of toast, like he was trying to charm him or something, like Teenie hadn't seen that smile pointed at a thousand chumps and lays over the years, like Teenie didn't know what it meant.

That smile exhausted him and he leaned deep into the shovel's handle, the wood so very smooth from years of use. "She loved you," he said again, the wonder of it flattening his voice.

And for a moment it looked like Ray got it, a tiny nod of his head, a shift of his eyes, but then he was talk-talking like always, some bullshit about love and loss, his tongue a rattler buzzing in Teenie's skull.

And Teenie thought of the tom, imagined putting him in the cabin of Ray's truck, saying, "It's okay, Holden," or something like that, before turning Ray's keys in the ignition. Before driving away, maybe leaving the amazing heat of a house on fire behind them.

The shovel's handle was smooth, almost silky against his fingers, and Teenie thought of the beautiful ache that would live in his shoulders if he swung. He stood up, pulling his heft off the soft, worked wood, and felt the weight of the shovel in every part of his tired back. And he held it up like that despite the pain, the head hovering just a little off the ground, his back straight as it would get, his tired body paralyzed by the thought of Ida, burnt up like leaves in a trash pile, curled in his mother's grave.

The Plague

When Cora caught the lawn guy smoking weed in the backyard instead of mowing, she wanted to say something cool, to ask for a drag or a hit or whatever you asked for if you were young and wonderful. She wanted to stand there next to him in the incredible heat and ponder the St. Augustine and dollarweed and cracked dirt and breathe it all in. But he was Al's kid, down the way, and so she did what she always did now. Nothing. She just stood there, dying of AIDS, and knocked on the widow to let him know she saw him, made him so scared she'd tell his dad that he fumbled the joint. She worried for a second it would set the yard on fire.

And then, watching the kid bend over looking for it, his low slung pants slinging ever lower, cool leaking out of him like helium pissing its way out of a balloon, Cora laughed.

There was a lesion on her scalp, an angry red mouth hiding under her hair, a reminder to be more diligent in taking the pills. Not that she ever forgot. She remembered and didn't take them anyway. Played roulette with the pills and jellybeans and little paper cups pilfered from Our Lady of Lourdes, a pair of red dice from Harrah's acted as the dark hand of fate.

When it had been her job to hand out pills, to visit the old syphilitic man in Maurice and the fat diabetic couple two streets over, the both of them with wounds that wouldn't heal—and even that cute bipolar cutter in Abbeville—back then, none of them wanted to take their meds. She'd never understood their reluctance. Had hated the way they all "forgot" on her days off, the way they'd clench their mouths like she might have to fight them, pry their stupid jaws open. She hated the way they seemed to want to march toward death and chaos instead of swallowing their damn medicine.

But she quit home health when she found out and became one of the marchers. "Fuck it," she told the doctor and went home and tried to stab her husband in the right lung for giving her the plague. She missed the lung, though. Maybe it was because he moved. Or maybe she didn't really want to kill him, to hear that sucking sound, to see the frothing blood. So she slid the knife below the lung and he lived.

The kid outside looked up, caught her laughing at him. She waved, wondering if his cupped hand meant he'd found the joint. She was amazed that his dad let him come over to mow, what with the cops and the plague and everything. Her face in *The Advertiser* that week. She'd even made it on the website: "Nurse Knifes Husband." The DA ended up being more sympathetic than you might imagine, the plague and the old bruises making her a pretty bad bet for his conviction rate. The paper never ran anything about her release.

She thought about offering the kid some lemonade. She had the powdered kind, pink, and was pretty sure there was ice. But he was pulling the string on the mower now—he used her ex's little pusher because his dad wouldn't let him drive the John Deere. She paid him forty dollars to do the whole yard, trim the edges and everything, but this was probably the last week for that. The ex not wanting to send her any more cash, the lawyer telling her to give up the ghost. To not spend the rest of her life fighting.

When she stopped paying him, the kid would be the last one to not come by her house anymore. And she'd be alone, not bothered by anyone, so that was good.

She mixed the lemonade and cracked a few shrunken ice cubes into a plastic Mardi Gras cup. Wondered which parade she'd caught it at. If the ex had caught it for her. She couldn't remember any of them anymore, the holes in her memory growing.

She made sure her hair was combed over the lesion, her nose clean and clear. She would make her mouth little, very little, to talk to him, keep her white tongue hidden, keep it all hidden.

"Hey, Mrs. Cora," the kid said, looking everywhere but at her when she showed up with the cup.

She meant to smile and say, "Look, Jamie, I'm not telling anyone. It's okay," but instead she told him about how the house had been crawling with spiders when they'd moved in a couple of years back "Black widows, wolf spiders, those are the brown jumpers, you know? Even recluses." She started coughing, wet and wheezy. Finally, "I'm pretty sure they were recluses."

The kid nodded.

The smell of marijuana and cut grass filled her up and she coughed it out. "Anyway, now we have the lizards."

He nodded again, like it made sense to him.

She wanted to stop talking about spiders, lizards, the yard, whatever. What she really wanted was to be sixteen with him, sixteen and alive and stoned. Anything but almost forty and dead. So she said, "Does your dealer deliver?" and watched him choke on the lemonade.

She started trading her pain pills for weed, but Cora didn't smoke it. She didn't exactly throw it away. She stored it. She emptied out the oregano shaker, the sage, the Herbs de Provence and slowly filled the pantry with the contents of the little sandwich bags Jamie's guy brought over. His guy, because, "No one has a dealer for crissake, it's not like real drugs."

She'd smoke with the guy though, with BD, her guy now too. If BD stayed and watched a little TV on the couch with her, packed a bowl in the glass pipe she bought from him, then she'd smoke.

"So, Jamie says you got the hivey." BD was paunchy and fuzzy, with freckles showing under his almost beard. She guessed he was maybe twenty-five years old. He lounged on her couch with his arms wide against the back, petting the microfiber a little. Completely comfortable.

"The what?" Cora looked at him. He didn't look like a dealer or someone's guy even. He looked like he'd make pizzas for a living. Like he'd show up in the ER with his knuckles blown to shit and a grin and a story about fireworks. A stoner guy, sure, but some hardcore dealer, no.

"The hivey. The hivs. The H-I-V." He passed her the little glass pipe, packed and ready. Fucking thing was pink and sparkly. "Cheerful," he'd called it.

Cora sucked in and waited for her teeth to itch. The first time she smoked, she told BD she hated the way her teeth felt. He laughed and told her she was one weird bitch. Now she waited for them to itch before she answered the question. "Full blown AIDS," she said finally, figuring why not tell this guy. Someone should know. "Rapid onset. It's rare, like I won the lottery."

"Fuck."

"Yeah. Jamie tell you I stabbed my husband?"

He shook his head, looked impressed. "Dick monkey gave it to you?"

"Yeah."

BD laughed, "Hope you shanked him good. You seen this episode?"

"No." Cora looked at him. "Not afraid you'll catch it from me?"

"Nah." It took him a while to say that, the one syllable a million miles long in his mouth. "My mom's a doctor. Besides my cousin's girl's sister had it and we got hi-igh all the time." He did this thing with his lips. A grimace, Cora guessed. "I hear we got more AIDS than like Africa here."

Cora touched the spot on her head with the lesion. There were two more now. "No, but a lot."

They watched the show for a while, a cop drama, BD laughing every time someone got smacked in the back of the head. "Not like you have to die from it now."

Cora nodded. The bad guy on the show got shot and his body flew backward, blood showing up when he hit the ground.

"You kill him?" he said.

She imagined doing it now. Going to his trailer and finding him, his body just a reservoir for the disease at this point, his virus load huge. She thought of him sitting there, all of the things the girls loved about him oozing out in the same thick mucus that made it hard for her to breathe. "No," she said.

BD shook his head, "It's a damn shame." They watched the guy on TV bleed a neat puddle onto the ground. A perfect squid of thick red stain. "Damn shame."

BD figured shooting the ex in the balls was the solution to all her problems, and he and Jamie would spend afternoons smoking up her house and talking about it. Their punishments getting ever more extreme, making her laugh pizza bits across the room. The two of them over a lot now.

When she asked him why they called him BD, he said, "I dated this girl in high school. She had a sense of irony," and laughed until he couldn't breathe, then couldn't even laugh proper, making a high pitched, girlie sound instead.

Cora raised her eyebrow.

"Big Dick," he finally got out and then she was laughing with him. The cough making it hard but still good.

She knew now that he was more than thirty, his fuzzy hair sliding backwards on his forehead, his stories of high school and some college told in that way so that you knew they were beginning to be blurry around the edges for him, bits smearing like stained photographs. One night after Jamie left, BD stayed late telling her those stories, but not the funny versions. The real ones. He told her how he got a girl pregnant in high school. How the girl's dad tried to have him arrested for statutory rape.

"But, you know I wasn't old enough. I'd lied when I told her I was eighteen." He shook his head, "She was the one who was older, right?" The girl miscarried, he said, and Cora knew that meant she had an abortion. He put his hand on her knee and left it there. Put his head on her shoulder after a while.

And she knew if things were different he'd just be a loser. But there was a rash the color of strawberries crawling across Cora's skin, eating her alive, and things weren't different.

But then a few days later Jamie showed up with his dad's gun, the fucking thing fat and black and shining. Him boosting it because everything sounds like a good idea when you're high and you're seventeen and someone else says it. And BD was always talking about how "if they just had a gun." Then things got really different.

They didn't make it to the ex's trailer, though. For a while they didn't make it anywhere, just sat in the living room, the guys smoking, her thinking she might bake them cookies or muffins, thinking of them as her boys.

Jamie had put the gun on the table and BD stared at it like a specimen, his hands on his knees, his nose close, but not too close, to the weapon.

"Damn, that's a big gun."

"It's a Judge." They were eating Cora's jellybeans. She had switched to just pills in the little paper cups, was taking all of them now, so she let them pick through the candy. Besides, there were no cookies or muffins coming. She didn't even have flour.

"That ain't for hunting."

Jamie laughed. "My dad don't hunt. Mostly, it's for show." He tried to pass his pipe to BD, but BD was transfixed by the gun.

"You ever shoot it?"

And they went on and on like that, Cora napping on the couch while they talked about the gun on the table. She wanted to tell them it was a stupid thing to have in the house, that Jamie's dad would fall out if he knew, that no one was shooting anyone, that she didn't care much one way or the other about the ex anymore. Instead she nodded. She laughed. She dozed. Too afraid if she spoke up they'd leave and not come back.

Finally sixteen again. Too stupid to speak up. So she got really high instead.

They would have stayed that way, maybe, high and running their mouths about the gun, doing nothing, if Cora hadn't got so very stoned.

But she did, and then she told them about how she was already dead.

How she just looked alive.

BD didn't laugh at that like he was supposed to. Instead, he said, "That fucker," touching the gun for the first time. The fascinated disgust gone now. "You're a good chick," he said. "Nice, you know," he said. "It isn't fair," he said, all the while his hand on that gun.

When Cora was a kid, her dad had a camp on Lake Maurepas. They would stay there on summer weekends, her folks fishing and drinking beer, her and her cousins swimming or skiing. For all she knew her dad still had it. They didn't talk much since her mom died. Her mom the glue between them. Cora never even told him about the AIDS.

The only air conditioning at the camp was window units in the two bedrooms, and the daytime temperatures reached all the way to 100 sometimes. So everyone stayed outside, catching little breezes off the water and swimming constantly, even at night. That was what she was thinking about when BD asked her where her ex lived now. Thinking about Lake Maurepas.

At night, you'd jump in the lake and it would be like a bath, not even cooled all the way off after the sun had long set. She loved that, how you slid in and the water was almost the same as the air, so your skin felt a lovely sort of confused. But that wasn't the best part.

Every time you moved, comb jellies would catch fire all around you, lighting up the murky water like blue fairy dust. Their soft bodies bumped you just a little, and everything was magic. Her mom told people it was weekends at the camp that made Cora want to study science, running around with alligators, frogs, comb jellies. She was proud of her science-y kid. But that wasn't really true. There, making slow figure eights to excite the little *Ctenophora*, there Cora believed only in magic.

"Maurepas," she said to BD, wanting more than anything to jump in with the jellies one last time. The doctor had told her that her that her CD4 T-cell count didn't look good on the last visit out. "You should have been taking the meds," he said. "You could have had years." They had known each other before she'd moved to home health, back when she worked in the hospital. They'd been close enough years ago that he was comfortable sounding pissed at her. Then he told her that he wanted to test her for signs of dementia. Cora just made a joke about looking for billboards in her brain.

"Maurepas," she said again.

Jamie whistled, "That's like three hours out. And it's late already." He checked his watch. "Almost eleven now."

But BD said, "That's not bad." His hand still on the Judge.

Jamie pointed out they were too fucked up to drive. The kid the only one saying anything useful, was not really paying the right sort of attention to the rest of it. She said something like, "It will be fine."

Somehow BD convinced Jamie, and the kid got in his Corolla, picking off paint flecks where it looked like the door had scraped a pole before getting in, like maybe he was still thinking he might not go. The guys sat in the front. Jamie's daddy's gun was tucked neatly into the waistband of BD's pants and no one pointed out how stupid that was, even as he shifted it around to get comfortable. Cora climbed in the back so she could stretch out her legs, keep the pressure off any one spot for too long. Her skin was such a mess there on the back of her thighs and calves.

She spent most of the drive flicking her mossy tongue against some sores in her mouth and thinking how Al wouldn't even let Jamie drive that John Deere to do lawns. Knowing that was an important fact, but not quite getting to why. Not even after she started to sober.

Mostly she wanted to feel the lake confusing her skin, so she didn't try real hard to figure anything else out.

BD lost some of his steam on the drive, but even after Cora admitted there was no need to shoot the ex, she got him to keep driving, watching Jamie's blond head bobble and nod from her spot in the backseat.

When he started to snore, it was a baby sound, and it kept right on when the flashing lights flickered behind them. It kept right on even when BD started saying "shit, shit, shit" under his breath and the car drifted sideways onto the shoulder.

From the back, Cora thought the cop lights looked just like the comb jellies, and she waved her fingers around a little, a sort of small figure eight.

BD was shifting in his seat, wiggling and contorting. "Shit, shit, shit," he said again and then, "Wake up. Take it. Take it, man."

Later she understood that BD was trying to get the Judge off his body before the cop got to the car: no guns on parole. But in the back seat, half-dreams lighting up her struggling synapsis, it seemed like a game, BD squirming, Jamie rubbing his eyes, putting his hands up, then shoving at BD, saying, "No way, no way." Just a game of hot potato.

But then Jamie said, "Get off me," his voice high, panicked, BD all over him. He opened the door, and for a second Cora thought they were still moving, that Jamie would slip into traffic, and she was suddenly very afraid. He slid out of the car backwards, his hands invisible, blocked by the seat until he fumbled, fell completely out, and Cora saw them through the window, empty and grasping at air, at the same time that the world cracked. A sharp blast and then ringing silence. A gunshot.

Her father was a hunter but she'd never heard a gun fired so close to her head. It was like diving into the water, the way sound changed when you hit the surface and, if you went far enough down, seemed to disappear completely, leaving only the rhythmic noise of your own blood buzzing past your ears.

Later she realized that BD didn't really know anything about handling a weapon, anyhow. That he should never have picked it up. That he'd shot Jamie in his panic. That he hadn't meant to.

But he had shot him.

Before the trial, BD would call, write, even knock on the door when he was out on bail and tell her over and over and over that the Judge went off in Jamie's hands. But she'd seen Jamie's hands as he fell backward out of the car, empty, holding nothing, just trying to right his body seconds before the cracking. Not after. Before.

In the car, though, in the car that night she understood none of it. Her ears hurt and she was shaking like mad. And when she looked out the window, there was such a mess. The sort of mess you saw in the ER only on the very worst nights. Little flecks of white bone or maybe gravel, maybe grass in the mess.

Jamie's thigh was not really a thigh anymore. His femoral artery spewing itself empty, and in her deafness Cora thought she heard the life hissing out of him. Even though he was on the ground outside the car. Even though she was pushed up against the glass of the window that separated them. She could hear him. This kid. This kid that did her lawn.

Direct pressure, she thought. I need to apply direct pressure.

But she didn't move.

I need to stick my hand in there. Clamp the artery. Stop the bleeding.

But she didn't move.

He was bleeding everywhere. There was no neat squid of thick red ink on the gravel. There was just that mess. Everywhere. She should check his vitals. Start compressions. He was going to bleed out.

She started to name the muscles, pectineus, sartorius, semimembranosus, semitendinosus, adductor magnus, adductor longus, adductor brevis, but she couldn't hear the words, just a high pitched whine.

Jamie dead in front of her. All bled out.

Cora alive but not moving. As still as Jamie. Al had let this boy, this almost man, his almost man come over. Mow her lawn. Al had not been afraid of her and her dying.

As the cop pulled her from the back seat, she saw that the bloom of Jamie's blood was so much darker than the rashes eating her away, so much darker than anything she'd ever seen.

Sometimes, when BD called, when the new home health nurse left, when she sat on the porch watching nothing, she would understand the ways it was her fault, her mind so thin around the edges, her thoughts like lace unraveling.

She was not sixteen. She was almost forty and she was dying, but not dead.

Acknowledgements

Thank you to my husband, Lee Rourks, without whom there would be no book, and to my mother, Kathy Moore, without whom I would never have had the courage to write a single sentence. You two are my heart.

And to the rest of the parental village: My papi, Robert "Bobby Jack" Camacho, who tells a tale better than anyone I know, Rosi Camacho, who showers me with love, and John Moore, who taught me to be strong and independent. To Marie Rourks, who practically adopted me and supports me as much as her own kid. And to Viviane and Juan Camacho, who I miss and think about every day. Y'all fill my life with love and stories.

Thank you to my tribe: Sharon Harrigan, who I emailed at least once a day, nearly every day to say whether I had written or not, who read almost every one of these stories, who held my hand through all of it; my "writing partner." Stephanie Bane, who knows my writing and voice better than I do and helps me find my path, who makes me laugh. And Deborah Reed, who walked first and put her hand out to pull me up behind her, who saw something in me I did not know I had. My girls.

And to Saul Lemerond and Rebecca Hazelwood who kept me breathing and writing and laughing through the PhD, who read my work, and who believed in me when I could not believe in myself. And who still do all that now. And to Arati "AJ" Jambotkar and Dusty Cooper who love me just the way I am.

To Eyatta Fischer my first best friend. My first writer friend. You are so very missed.

Thank you to Jack Bedell, Benjamin Percy, Bonnie Jo Campbell, Pam Houston, Craig Lesley, Hilma Wolitzer, John McNally, B. K. Loren, and all the other teachers and mentors who held me up. And to Pacific University, Writing by Writers, and the Key West Literary Seminar for introducing me to most of these great humans.

A special thanks to Nicole Bertone, who answered medical questions for me, and Brian Lashua, who answered legal ones. All mistakes are my own.

And finally thank you to the journals and editors who first published these works in slightly different forms. "Moon Trees" first appeared in *Prairie Schooner*, "Everything Shining" in the anthology *American Fiction: Volume 13*, "Shallowing" in *TriQuarterly*, "Deformed," in *Pembroke Magazine*, "Clown" in *Spilt Infinitive*, "The Revival" in *PANK*, "At the Very End" in *Passing Through Journal*, "Pinched Magnolias" in *The Greensboro Review*, "El Feo" in the anthology *Tudor Close*, "Pulpo" in *SmokeLong Quarterly*, and "The Plague" in *Kenyon Review Online*. And to Diane Goettel for giving the book a great home.

Photo: Lety Remior

Leigh Camacho Rourks is a Cuban-American author who lives and works in Central Florida, where she is an Assistant Professor of English and Humanities at Beacon College. She is the recipient of the St. Lawrence Press Award, the Glenna Luschei Prairie Schooner Award, and the Robert Watson Literary Review Prize, and her work has been shortlisted for several other awards. Her fiction, poems, and essays have appeared in a number of journals, including *Kenyon Review, Prairie Schooner, RHINO, TriQuarterly, December Magazine,* and *Greensboro Review.*

CPSIA information can be obtained
at www.ICGtesting.com
Printed in the USA
LVHW111446020822
725010LV00016B/144